W9-BIX-531

GUSTAV GLOOM

AND THE INN OF SHADOWS

by Adam-Troy Castro
illustrated by Kristen Margiotta

Grosset & Dunlap
An Imprint of Penguin Group (USA) LLC

GROSSET & DUNLAP
Published by the Penguin Group
Penguin Group (USA) LLC, 375 Hudson Street, New York, New York 10014, USA

USA | Canada | UK | Ireland | Australia | New Zealand | India | South Africa | China

penguin.com
A Penguin Random House Company

Text copyright © 2015 Adam-Troy Castro. Illustrations copyright © 2015 Kristen Margiotta. All rights reserved. Published by Grosset & Dunlap, a division of Penguin Young Readers Group, 345 Hudson Street, New York, New York 10014. GROSSET & DUNLAP is a trademark of Penguin Group (USA) LLC. Manufactured in China.

Book design by Christina Quintero. Typeset in MrsEaves, Neutraface, and Strangelove Text.

Library of Congress Cataloging-in-Publication Data is available.

ISBN 978-0-448-46458-9   10 9 8 7 6 5 4 3 2 1

This one's for Hillary Pearlman,

because that designation makes this book

a work of art for a work of art who wears

a work of art and makes a work of art;

how artful is that?

CHAPTER ONE
THE GIRL WHO LOOKED A LOT LIKE FERNIE WHAT BUT WHO STILL WASN'T FERNIE WHAT

Despite what we're so frequently shown in movies, not all of life's worst news arrives on a dark and stormy night, with thunder and lightning for company.

Some terrible news arrives on glorious sunny days, sometimes even in the well-lit kitchens of Fluorescent Salmon houses.

For instance, outside the home of the What family, the light was bright and golden, the grass lush and green. The air rang with the joyful melodies of birdsong and the distant laughter of neighborhood children. All was right with the world.

Inside the house, the famous world adventurer Nora What stood reading a very strange and frightening letter from her missing ten-year-old daughter, Fernie.

Mrs. What had just returned from one of

her frequent televised expeditions and was still dressed in a safari jacket, jodhpurs, and a pith helmet. She wore a necklace of lions' teeth she'd been given by local tribesmen impressed by her skill at evading crocodiles in a swim across a river most sensible people avoided because it almost had more crocodiles than water. (The local tribesmen generally resisted engaging in such pointlessly risky activities themselves and considered Nora What insane and stupid for doing what they quite sensibly would not. But they'd learned from past exposures to self-proclaimed adventurers that the best way to get rid of a crazy person in a pith helmet was to praise her for her bravery and give her a ceremonial necklace of some kind and thus some reason to think she'd accomplished something of note.)

On her return home, Mrs. What had expected to be met at the airport by her husband and her daughters, ten-year-old Fernie and twelve-year-old Pearlie. She'd made this arrangement with her husband just three weeks earlier. The trip to pick her up was going to be a surprise for the girls. But her family hadn't been at the airport when she got off the plane. They hadn't answered the phone, nor had they been at home when Mrs. What arrived in front of the new house in a taxi.

Mrs. What supposed that they might have had car trouble, forgotten the date, or gone out on some unexpected errand, but the family cat, Harrington, was missing, too, and it was difficult for her to imagine an unexpected errand that could possibly require the participation of a cat.

All of this had been extremely disturbing to Mrs. What, who despite her frequent and lengthy professional absences loved her family and liked being able to come home to them.

Still, it had not been anywhere near as disturbing as the letter Mrs. What had just read, not once but five times.

Mrs. What wasn't sure that she was supposed to believe what she read.

Fernie had written that the spooky house across the street was inhabited by shadows that walked and talked and had lives of their own.

She went on to explain that it also contained the Pit, a gateway to a strange otherworldly realm called the Dark Country. The homeland of all shadows, it was at war with an evil conqueror named Lord Obsidian, which was admittedly exactly the kind of name Mrs. What supposed

3

was appropriate for the kind of person who made war with dark countries.

Mrs. What's husband and her older daughter, Pearlie, had somehow fallen into the Pit and would never be seen again unless rescued. Fernie's letter concluded with the news that she'd taken Harrington the cat and joined the house's one somewhat human resident, a strange boy named Gustav Gloom, on an expedition with exactly that purpose in mind.

Fernie had written all of this in just a couple of pages, rushing through a complicated story that probably would have required three full-length illustrated books to tell and still left a lot unexplained.

Mrs. What wasn't sure that further details would have rendered the story any more comprehensible, but they might have helped.

When there's a pile of questions fighting to be asked, the first one to escape is sometimes the best.

Mrs. What wondered out loud, "Exactly how old is this letter, anyway?"

A voice that sounded just like Fernie's replied, "Fernie wrote it about eight days ago."

While it struck Mrs. What as distinctly odd

that Fernie would refer to herself using her own name, the relief she felt that this nonsense about shadow houses and dark countries was all over and done with was overwhelming. She spun in her chair, a big broad smile on her face.

Then she faltered.

The room was inhabited by shadows. Not the kind of shadows that were normally present in the corners of rooms, but actual active presences who had been standing around behind Mrs. What, waiting for her to finish reading Fernie's letter.

One was a hulking figure in a tuxedo, another a lanky man wearing a striped suit and a flat straw hat, and a third looked enough like Fernie to make Mrs. What's heart ache. She had Fernie's eyes and Fernie's nose and Fernie's chin and pretty much everything else Fernie had except for the bright red hair—which wasn't to say that this girl was bald, only that her hair looked more like what red hair looks like in black-and-white photographs.

It would have been all too tempting for Mrs. What to still believe that this actually was Fernie in some way . . . but Mrs. What was an attentive and loving mother in between her frequent expeditions, and she could tell from the way the little girl carried herself that she was not Fernie at all, but a different person who just happened to look like her.

Mrs. What could only say so. "You're not Fernie."

"I didn't say I was," the little girl shadow replied.

"But you talk like her. You have her voice."

"I'm her shadow. How else would you expect me to sound?"

Mrs. What, who had seen her share of astonishing sights, had not seen anything quite this astonishing for as far back as she could remember. "I didn't expect *you* to have a voice at all."

The shadow girl sniffed. "All shadows have voices. But we just don't speak that much around people from the world of light."

Mrs. What didn't know what to say. "Ummm. I'm sorry?"

The hulking figure rolled his eyes. "That's exactly the kind of answer that makes flesh-and-blood people so often not worth my valuable time."

"You'll have to forgive Hives," said the shadow

of the man in the striped suit and straw hat. "He's the Gloom house's terrible butler. It's his job to always be rude to the people who need his help."

"He seems to be awfully good at it," Mrs. What noted.

"I'm a professional," sniffed Hives.

"As for me," said the man in the straw hat, "I'm the shadow of a fellow named Mr. Notes, who last I checked wasn't a very nice man at all, but I don't follow him around anymore and I'm trying to be a much more pleasant person. I hope we'll be good friends."

One of the many pressing questions piling up in Mrs. What's head, so deep by now that it was a wonder she had room to think at all, squirmed out from underneath. She addressed it to the shadow girl. "If you're Fernie's shadow, aren't you supposed to be with her?"

"I'm a free being. I can be wherever I want to be."

"But you're *usually* with her, aren't you?"

"Yes," Fernie's shadow said, "I am, but that's a matter of choice, and it's because I like her." With a faint note of disapproval, she added, "Personally, I think you should spend more time with her yourself."

"Why aren't you with her now?"

"Well, I do tend to stick very close to Fernie, but then a little while back, when she was being chased by a shadow dinosaur, I got stomped on and jammed up between his toes."

Suddenly, swimming with crocodiles seemed very mundane to Mrs. What. "Does that kind of thing happen often?"

"Where Fluffy the tyrannosaur is concerned? Unfortunately, yes. They're not toes you want to get yourself stuck between. They smell like rotten bananas dipped in rancid mayonnaise and stored in a sweaty gym sock. I don't know why they call that big lummox 'Fluffy' when he should be called 'Stinky' instead."

Mrs. What felt the room spinning. "Losing a little control of your story, aren't you?"

"I suppose. Anyway, it normally takes a shadow no time at all to recover from being crushed flat or to get out from under heavy objects like dinosaur toes, but I wasn't the only shadow Fluffy stomped in that crowded hallway, and his feet were sticky, so we all got mixed together in a kind of jam. When we fell off, it was all in one big lump, like hard candies melted together in a bowl. A very bad shadow named Ursula recovered a couple of seconds before the rest of us did and had the time to lock me away in what I suppose you would call a closet, where I remained imprisoned until Gustav's shadow, who was looking for me by that point, heard my cries and let me out."

Mr. Notes's shadow took over the story. "Yes. You see, Mrs. What, Fernie's friend Gustav had sent his shadow to find Fernie's shadow, but by the time he succeeded in that mission, Fernie had already left with Gustav to rescue your husband and older daughter from the Dark Country."

The strangeness of this encounter had overwhelmed Mrs. What so much that until this last sentence she'd almost managed to forget that they were talking about the fate of her family. "The letter says . . . they fell into a pit of some kind?"

Hives sniffed. "Your husband's clumsy."

This was the first part of the story Mrs. What couldn't even begin to argue with. "And . . . Gustav and Fernie have gone there to rescue them?"

"Uh-huh," said Fernie's shadow. "Word around the house has it that they must have taken the Cryptic Carousel."

Mrs. What didn't know what a Cryptic

Carousel was, but it struck her as the kind of detail that instantly grants believability to unbelievable stories. Without wanting to, she suddenly found herself certain that everything Fernie had written about in her letter, all that nonsense about a house filled with shadows and a pit down to the country all shadows came from and so on, was absolutely true. The awfulness of this revelation welled up in her like a storm, leaving her frantic in the manner that only a terrified mother can be frantic. She leaped to her feet and made the chair fall over behind her and clatter on the kitchen floor like angry applause. "Oh . . . *my family!*"

Fernie's shadow bit her shadow lip. "I know it's upsetting. I'm still not entirely sure that telling you was better than *not* telling you, but I figured that Fernie would want you informed, so we've kept an eye on your house, hoping to scoot on over here and give you the heads-up if you came home."

"What . . . what should I do?"

"That's a very good question," said Fernie's shadow.

"You think so?" asked Hives. "It strikes me as a wholly average question."

"It's relevant and to the point," Mr. Notes's shadow argued.

"Oh, I recognize that," Hives allowed. "I wouldn't call it a bad question, either. But it's not as brilliantly incisive as you're painting it. I wouldn't give this woman credit for asking a 'very good' question yet."

Mrs. What had suffered more than enough of this. *"I wasn't asking your opinion of the question. I was asking you to answer the question! What do I have to do to get my family back?"*

The shadow of Mrs. What's younger daughter surprised her by crossing the distance between them and placing one gray hand on the back of hers. The comforting touch felt cool, like a piece of silk, but aside from the temperature it was so much like Fernie's touch that Mrs. What felt her heart break a little at the thought that this could be all she had left.

"This is the problem," Fernie's shadow said. "I'm really not all that sure that there's much we can do."

"You mean it's hopeless?"

"No. Nothing's ever hopeless. But there isn't much you *can* do, is my point. There's no purpose in informing the police of your world that your family's gone missing, because they'll never believe your story about where your family's gone and would only waste time looking in all the places in your world where we already know your family isn't. You can't go down to the Dark Country yourself looking for them, because the only way for you to get there now that the Carousel's gone is to jump into the Pit yourself, and that'll more than likely only deliver you to Lord Obsidian and make you yet another person Gustav and Fernie will need to rescue . . . and trust me, they already have plenty of those."

All of this made a crazy kind of sense, even if it also made no sense whatsoever. Mrs. What, who was normally brilliant at dealing with emergencies and had once survived a week buried alive by an avalanche using nothing but a teapot, a hand mirror, and a fountain pen, now found herself paralyzed with fear. "But I can't just sit here and do nothing! My children—"

"—are not helpless," Mr. Notes's shadow finished. "Yes, they're in more trouble than any person of flesh should ever have to face, but if you knew the kind of dangers they've already braved, and the kind of monsters they've already defeated, you'd be more proud of your girls than you've ever been before."

Mrs. What was proud of her girls already, but still didn't find this very comforting.

The shadow girl paused now, to give her next words a weight that even a distraught mother had to feel. "And then you also have to consider Gustav."

"I'm sure he's a very brave little boy, but—"

Fernie's shadow took offense at that. "He's more than just brave, more than just the best friend Fernie has ever had or ever will have. He's half shadow himself, almost as fast and cunning and hard to kill as a shadow—a good thing, as he's spent all his life in a wondrous place facing down more dangers than even you could possibly imagine. If you knew the things he's already done and the things he is prepared to do in defense of your family, then you'd know that your girls and husband are in the hands of the best possible companion. If anybody can get them home alive, it's him."

The certainty in the shadow girl's voice was like nothing Mrs. What had ever heard. It was the kind of faith she would have liked to have in a friend—the kind so great that it banished all doubt.

Maybe that made her feel a little better . . . but a little was not nearly enough. She was a woman who faced dangers on her own rather than allowing others to face them for her, and it was difficult for her to endure being told, by a shadow no less, that there was nothing she could do.

Struggling to remind herself that this strange thing really did seem to be happening and was not just some terrible dream brought on by airline food, she protested, "But I can't just stay here and pretend nothing's happened. I'll go crazy. I have to be able to do *something*."

The shadow girl's features softened, showing compassion that was so much like the way Fernie would have, it was all Mrs. What could do just to avoid breaking into tears. "I'm sorry. I really can't think of anything useful."

"Maybe there's someone else I can talk to?"

"There are plenty of other shadows you can talk to, but not many who'd answer you, or agree to get involved, or give you the kind of help you want. Great-Aunt Mellifluous is down in the Dark Country herself, helping to lead the battle against Lord Obsidian. Gustav's shadow already dived into the Pit himself to try to catch up with them. Hives, here, has duties in the house that he needs to get back to. Mr. Notes's shadow . . ." She hesitated and apologized to him. "I'm sorry, he's a good friend, but just isn't the most useful person to have around in a crisis."

"I'm not," Mr. Notes's shadow apologized. "I panic too easily."

Fernie's shadow continued: "Hieronymus Spector is a villain who would lead you nowhere but ruin. And Fluffy, for all his good points, has never been the brightest bulb in the pack. He's helpful when you want to break something, not so helpful when it comes to giving advice."

These names meant nothing to Mrs. What, but she gathered that none of the individuals mentioned would be able or willing to help. "Isn't there anybody else?"

"Anybody else would either ignore you or try to make matters worse for you. I'm sorry, but try as I might, I can't think of even one other shadow we could turn to . . ."

"Then you're not thinking very hard," a new voice said. "I know a shadow who can help."

It wasn't actually a new voice, but a very familiar one.

It was the voice of a healthy woman in her early forties, a voice that Mrs. What knew exactly as well as she knew her own.

Mrs. What whirled again, realizing as she did that she was certainly doing a lot of that today. She found herself facing a shadow exactly her height, wearing the same kind of safari jacket and jodhpurs and pith helmet she wore; a shadow who presented herself as being slightly younger than she was, but still wore a face Mrs. What knew from seeing it in the mirror every morning.

"I volunteer," her shadow said.

What happened next was not a typical thing for Mrs. Nora What.

She was an intrepid and world-famous explorer and adventurer. She climbed mountains blindfolded, she swam with crocodiles, she kayaked off the edges of towering waterfalls, and she tickled sharks. She had done any number of things just because she'd been dared to do them, and had never once run away from a challenge in fear.

But she had also already received several upsetting shocks in the last few minutes, shocks that completely disturbed her understanding of the way the world worked and had shaken her even more than she'd realized.

The second her own shadow spoke to her, she did something she had never done before.

Nora What, fearless explorer and adventurer, fainted.

CHAPTER TWO
MORE OR LESS "MEANWHILE . . ."

If Nowhere could be an actual place, it would look just like the wastelands that surrounded the Dark Country. They were just a flat, colorless emptiness, extending in all directions and not worth noting at all if not for the vast ring of mountains at its center, which enclosed the true home of all shadows. Every other direction was just a featureless straight line, without so much as a pebble or blade of grass. Had there been a gopher hole anywhere, it would have been the most spectacular sight for miles.

A long line of dispirited shadows marched away from the Dark Country and into that featureless distance. There were thousands of them, maybe tens of thousands. A few had easily distinguishable faces, but the majority had never been the shadows of specific people and so were just vague shapes, blurry at the edges and hard to assign pasts and personalities. But even so, it was easy to see, just from the hopeless way they trudged and the hopeless way they wept, that they were just like refugees anywhere, in that they were shattered and heartbroken at having been forced to flee the now war-torn land they had known as home. They were beings with nowhere to go, who were forced to go there anyway.

This was an odd place to imagine anybody ever staging a joyous reunion.

But ten-year-old Fernie What, who had traveled across worlds and braved terrible dangers to reach this very spot, had just found her missing twelve-year-old sister, Pearlie, and for the last several minutes the two girls had not been able to stop hugging each other over and over again.

Gustav Gloom, who was always dressed in an impeccable black suit with a red tie, had already been pulled into a couple of those hugs, still a novel experience for him since he'd been raised by shadows and hadn't experienced the normal human allotment of embraces. (He still wasn't very comfortable with them, but had come around to believing that they might not be entirely a bad thing.) He'd had enough of them for the moment, but knew the girls weren't done with theirs, and so left them to their privacy while he returned to the parade of strangers. He addressed those passing by: "Excuse me? Anybody here willing to tell me what's happening?"

One of the nearest shadows, an ancient figure with a nose like a bedspring and a neck that had three separate bends in it before it reached his oddly shaped head, slowed down enough to mutter, "What does it look like, boy? We're all *running away*."

"To what? What's out there but more nothingness?"

"At least out there Lord Obsidian won't be able to do what he wants with us."

"Which is what?" Gustav asked. "If you're shadows and can't be killed, what could he have done that would make you all frightened enough to run away?"

The shadow refugee just shuddered and walked on.

Gustav hustled to keep up. "Please, sir. I know I'm just a halfsie boy and your kind usually doesn't like mine, but I'm not trying to be cruel.

I have to go into the Dark Country to rescue my father, and I really need to know. Just what does Lord Obsidian do to shadows that makes him so terrible that so many would rather run away than face him?"

The refugee stopped midstep and slowly turned to face Gustav. His features came into focus, revealing him to be the shadow of a very angry young man with burning red eyes that only escaped being terrifying because of the odd shape of the nose between them.

He jabbed a long gnarled finger at Gustav's nose and said, "You're wrong about one key thing, halfsie boy. It only used to be true that shadows couldn't die. That monster's smart enough to have built weapons that can destroy us. Weapons of science and magic both that can erase us where we stand, and have already erased more of us than can possibly be numbered. Don't you dare say we can't be killed. Lord Obsidian— may his name be cursed ten thousand times— has already demonstrated that we can be."

Gustav was so stunned that he fell a step back. "I . . . didn't know."

"And even that's not the worst of it," the refugee continued, each jab of his finger driving

Gustav another step back. "If it were just death coming to take away home and everything we've ever had, even the cowards among us would stand and fight. We would fight even though he's come up with more devilment than any peaceful shadow should ever have to face. We would fight even though he has secrets that can turn living men into shadows, others that can carry his foul minions from place to place in less time than it takes to think it, and others still like shadow eaters and worse that make opposing him a certain path to the end of us. But none of that's the worst of it, boy. None of that's the worst, at all; none of that's the reason the ones you see have run away."

Gustav stopped his retreat midstep and let the latest finger jab against his chest dissolve into a puff of gray smoke. "Okay. So what is?"

The angry shadow seemed to deflate all at once. "The one thing we've seen him do to his shadow enemies . . . that is far more frightening to us than mere death."

"What?" asked Gustav.

The shadow walked away, and before Gustav could follow him, he had melded with the crowd and become impossible to find against all the other gray figures trudging off into the emptiness.

There are times when even a boy who's been raised in a house filled with monsters and dangerous rooms is capable of feeling a knot of fear at the pit of his belly, and this was one of them.

He might have found another refugee to question to learn what "more frightening to us than mere death" meant, but then something else occurred to him and he ran back to the two What girls, who when he found them had just noticed his absence and were scanning the crowd to find him.

The determined young Fernie and the somewhat traumatized Pearlie looked—accurately—like it had been a while since they'd last been on the same planet as a comb. Both girls were redheads and pale by nature, but Pearlie's time trapped in the Dark Country, away from the sun, had rendered her skin even paler, hiding a number of her compensatory freckles and making her almost as ghostly white as Gustav.

Gustav demanded of her, "Pearlie! Where's your shadow?"

The older What sister looked down at the ground at Gustav's feet. "Where's yours?"

"Mine's accounted for," Gustav said quickly. "I left him at home. We don't know where Fernie's shadow has gotten off to, but she seems to be back at my house, too. But, Pearlie, the last thing I remember your shadow doing, just after you fell into the Pit, was diving in to join you. Why isn't *she* still with you? I need to know."

Pearlie took a deep breath and, very quietly, sank to the ground. For a moment it looked like all the strength had gone out of her legs. But no; she simply had a long story to tell, and it was too hard a story to remember without letting the ground support her. "She went with him when the minions got him."

"Tell us what happened."

She closed her eyes and said, "It was, I don't know, a couple of days after we landed in the Dark Country. It was very unpleasant and very gray, and it was sometimes very hard to figure out what we were looking at. I don't remember it as being very fun at all. It was just scary, and . . . well, scary, and—"

"Got it," Gustav snapped. "Scary. What next?"

Pearlie seemed taken aback at his impatience. "Well, after a while we found a . . . cave, I guess you'd call it. The only reason I'm not sure that's what it was is that the walls had these weird spiky things on them, and it always sounded like somebody was trapped farther down, mumbling to himself about a defective jet pack. We never did find out what that had to do with anything.

"After a while, Dad told me to stay inside and wait for him while he went out looking for something we could use to start a fire. I didn't see why, because we weren't cold. We weren't really warm or cold. But Dad said it was very important to start a fire. He insisted that starting a fire was the thing to do in a situation like this. He said it was the first instruction in all the safety manuals."

Fernie shook her head. "It's the first thing to do when you're lost in the woods, not when lost in the Dark Country."

"I kept telling him that, Fernie. But you know Dad. He insisted that certain principles were universal. 'When you're lost,' he said, 'you're always best off doing what the official guidelines say.' I pointed out that looking for wood was going to be a hard thing to do since we hadn't seen any trees yet, but he said that there were always trees, and as far as he was concerned that settled it."

She seemed about to start crying, but bit it back, and told the next bit in a voice very cold, very angry, and very controlled.

"I was watching from a distance when they came down from the sky on what looked like ropes. There were a couple dozen of them . . . all very big and bulky and stupid, the shadows of the kind of people who aren't happy unless they're pushing other people around. They carried shadow weapons that looked like swords. Dad kept running from one to the other, looking for a gap so he could break free. One snatched Dad's shadow away from his body and stuffed it in a little box, hooting, 'You won't need this helpful fella where you're going!' Another cried, 'Ooooh, now. Look at the warmbody, thinks he can boss around the likes of us. He'll be a grand one for our lord's mines.'

"Another one laughed nastily and said, 'You might even be lucky and not go into the mines at all. If you're deserving, our lord also knows how to turn one of your kind into one of ours. It's painful, and he'll only do it if he thinks you'll be useful, but when he's done, you'll fit in with the rest of us. Just look at me! I used to be a man meself. Just not a very good man.'"

Pearlie's hands curled into fists. "Dad cursed them. He called them names and tried to tackle them and told them they would pay. He never gave them a single reason to think he was afraid, and they thought it was funny until he also said, 'Gustav and Fernie will stop you.'"

Gustav said, "I bet that made them stop laughing."

"It did, Gustav. I didn't understand why, but it did."

"I have a reputation," he explained. "And Fernie's getting one."

"I found that out later, while traveling with this bunch." Pearlie waved at the mob of refugees filing back behind them. "They aren't the friendliest folks in the whole world—it's like you said, Gustav; most shadows don't seem to care whether humans live or die—but a couple of them were chatty enough to ask me my name, and when I told them, word traveled quickly up and down the line. You're famous down here for being the grandson of Lemuel and the son of Hans, and also for being the boy to defeat the shadow eater. Even Fernie's famous for being your sidekick."

This latest revelation made Fernie yelp. *"Excuse me!?!"*

Gustav's stern expression softened with confusion. "What?"

"I'm not Robin the Boy Wonder! I'm not Chewbacca or Ron Weasley or Doctor John H. Watson, MD! I'm not a sidekick!"

"But I didn't call you a sidekick," Gustav protested. "That's just what the shadows called you."

"Well, we're going to have to set the record straight as soon as we're done fixing everything else! Getting a reputation as a sidekick is just plain unacceptable!"

"I know," Gustav said. "That's why I call you a friend."

Fernie's mouth slammed shut with a click and she looked away, a little ashamed of herself.

Pearlie returned to her story in a hurry to avoid getting sidetracked by any further arguments over proper billing. "Anyway, as soon as Dad mentioned the two of you, the shadows got very excited. One said, 'Oi, now. Do you know who we have, laddies? This must be the father of those What brats! Our lord's taken a special interest in your lot! Why, it wasn't all that long ago that he sent his People Taker and a small army of shadows up to the world of light just to capture you! Am I right?'

"Dad did that thing he does with his chin when he's really mad. 'Yes, sir, you're right. And do you know what happened to the People Taker when he tried?'

"The minion gave him a long snotty look. 'Well, you're here, aren't you?'

"Dad said, 'That's right, I am. But that has nothing to do with anything the People Taker did. It only happened because I'm a clumsy man. Ask anybody. I'm always breaking glasses, tripping over things, and tumbling into bottomless pits. I've caught my hand in more doors than you'll find in some entire neighborhoods. It's why I became a safety expert in the first place. I have to be.

"'But my little girls,' he said, 'and their friend Gustav? They've beaten the People Taker twice and the shadow eater once. What does that tell you about starting fights with my family?'"

Pearlie bit her lip. "He included me to fool them, to keep them from realizing that I was only a few feet away, hiding and helpless.

"They looked around, frightened, not knowing what to do. For a moment it looked like they might let him go. But then they moved toward him, cackling.

"That's when my own shadow whispered to me.

"She hasn't spoken to me as much as your shadows have spoken to you, but she spoke to me then. She said, 'I'm going to him,' and left me behind as she slipped away. The next thing I knew she was out in the middle of them, flying at their faces and making them scatter. But it was too little too late. One grabbed her by the arm and stuffed her down into his sack, muttering something about stupid little girl shadows who don't mind their own business."

Pearlie trembled. "I half expected them to come after me next, but they didn't even look. It was like . . . they thought I wasn't even worth the trouble of looking for."

Gustav put his hand on hers. "They didn't think anything like that. They would have taken you if they'd known you were there. But the Dark Country's the land all shadows come from, the land where they walk around by themselves all the time. As long as your shadow kept quiet about you, no minion catching her would have had any reason to suspect that the girl whose shape she wore was also within their reach." He thought about that for a minute. "Are you sure that's what she said, though? 'I'm going to him'? Not, 'I'm going to rescue him' or 'I'll be right back'? But 'I'm going to him'?"

"That's what she said," Pearlie insisted. "'I'm going to him.' And then she tried to chase them off."

Gustav nodded to himself, and for just a moment didn't seem to be looking at Fernie or Pearlie or even the dreary landscape around them, but at some conveyor built inside his own head, where things that didn't make sense got fed into a machine and came out reshaped as things that did.

Finally he said, "She *meant* to be captured and taken with him to Lord Obsidian."

Pearlie said, "Yes."

Gustav still didn't know what the shadows considered more frightening than death, but comforted himself now with the knowledge that, at the bare minimum, Pearlie's shadow had not suffered it the last time she'd been seen.

He said, "Good."

CHAPTER THREE
"MERRY" IS NOT A WORD THAT COMES UP MUCH

Fernie What had faced unmentionable dangers alongside her best friend, Gustav Gloom. She'd traveled to other worlds with him. She trusted him with her life and the lives of her family. But every once in a while he said something so clueless or infuriating that she just had to yell at him. Now she stiffened with anger at the cold cruelty Gustav had just unexpectedly shown. She joined her sister in crying, *"Good!?!?"*

Gustav seemed to realize that he'd given offense, and he hastened to explain. "Come on. I don't mean it's *good* that she was captured. It's good that she went willingly. It means we'll have an ally waiting once we catch up."

Fernie didn't see how that necessarily followed. "It also means that we have to go up against Lord Obsidian's slave catchers and not be caught ourselves. That's *much* better."

Gustav surprised her by saying, "Yes, Fernie. It is."

"What?"

"I'd much rather know exactly where I'm going and who I'm fighting than have to spend forever searching for one missing man in the middle of a place as large as the Dark Country."

"But they'll—"

Gustav was in far too much of a hurry to be kind about it. "Yes, they'll probably be very mean to him. That's just the way evil minions act. It's never been the kind of profession that attracts nice people. I'm sorry, but that's true."

The two girls drew close, unable to bear the prospect of what their poor father must have been enduring.

"But," Gustav said, "they'll also want to make sure they deliver him to Lord Obsidian in prime condition, and that's good news, too. For a little while, at least, he's better off in their hands than he would be wandering around the Dark Country with no idea where he is. It just means that all we have to do is catch up."

"And defeat them," Fernie said, for the

moment not feeling much hope, "and rescue him, and manage to get away, and on top of all that arrange for our trip home."

"Aside from also finding and rescuing my own dad as long as we're here, that's pretty much the plan." Gustav had made it sound no worse than a trip to the supermarket to get a fresh carton of milk. He turned to Pearlie. "It's up to you whether you want to come along. After all, you've already escaped the Dark Country once. Entering it a second time, and hoping to escape with your life a second time, might be a little too much to ask of anyone."

Pearlie surveyed the emptiness of the land around them, taking in all the nothing surrounded by nothing on top of nothing with a nice extra added helping of nothing on top. "What do you expect me to do instead? Stay here forever?"

"Well, not *forever*. We'll be sure to come back to get you as soon as we're done rescuing everybody. We probably won't be able to get word back to you about how we're doing, but at least you'd be safe, in the meantime."

Pearlie shuddered. "And worrying about you and Fernie every second."

"I didn't promise it would be perfect, Pearlie. I just said it would be *safe*."

Poor Pearlie looked like what she was: a young girl being asked to make an impossible decision.

Fernie knew how trapped Pearlie must feel and dearly wished there were some way to talk her older sister into staying behind. After all, it would leave her with one less person to worry about. But she also knew that Pearlie was just as trapped by her own duty as a big sister and could not watch Fernie march into the Dark Country without going along herself to help.

There was only one decision Pearlie could make. The awfulness of it could be measured by just how long it took her to speak. "Gustav, if it's a choice between being *safe* but having nothing else to do but worry for who knows how long or being in danger every moment but at least being with you guys *doing something*, I'd rather be with you guys *doing something*. If that's okay with you."

"It's okay with me. *If* it's okay with you. You've been through a lot."

Pearlie glanced back in the direction of the terrible place she'd escaped, to which she was now expected to return. "I'll go."

"Good," said Gustav. "The more the merrier, I always say."

A terrible cloud passed over Pearlie's freckled features. "I just came from the Dark Country, Gustav. *Merry* isn't a word that you should expect to come up much."

"I don't see why not," said Gustav, as always insisting on optimism even as his mouth continued to form a thin, sad line. "Places are only as terrible as the people you find there, and wherever we go together, it'll always still be *us*."

It wasn't much to hold on to, not in this place, but Fernie had no other choice but to try. Beside her, Pearlie nodded as well. They both knew the worst was still coming, and they were both ready to face it.

Gustav stood and turned his attention back to the long line of shadow refugees, which had spent the last several minutes continuing to trudge by without paying much attention to the three friends from the land of light. There were so many of them that for the most part they looked like a long gray trickle, flowing down the side of the mountain to become a full-size river. A few could be distinguished as the shapes of people, and these were heartbreaking, because they were people without hope, people who had already seen the worst that they ever should have been expected to see.

He shouted, "Excuse me! Everybody! May I have your attention please? I want to talk to all of you about something very important."

Not all of the refugee shadows stopped to pay attention to Gustav. Many just lowered or shook their heads and kept on trudging into the distant emptiness. But a few slowed and turned toward him, showing less interest in what he had to say than resignation that here was yet another interruption arriving just in time to make the day even less pleasant.

The audience wasn't nearly large enough, but he shouted again. "You all know who I am—I'm Gustav Gloom, grandson of Lemuel and son of Hans. My family's opposed the man who became Lord Obsidian since long before I was born."

A thin, reedy voice emerged from the crowd. "Didn't stop him while you had the chance, though, did you?"

Gustav was a trifle slowed by this reasonable point, but after a moment he rallied and recovered. "No, we didn't. And maybe we should have before he became so powerful. But that doesn't mean I'm willing to quit, either. I'm perfectly willing to face him if I have to. You know what that says?"

"That you're stupid?" the same voice suggested.

There was a rumble of nasty laughter. The crowd seemed to grow darker and denser, as if Gustav's success at offending them gave them back some of the substance they may have given up by running away from a fight.

This didn't discourage Gustav. "My friends and I are headed into the Dark Country to rescue our fathers. I don't expect all of you to join us; I know that you have just spent a whole lot of effort running *away* from there. But if any of you feel any shame over *having* to give up your homes and run, then maybe one or two of you will stand with us as we do what needs to be done."

There was more angry muttering from shadows who did not much appreciate being mocked by this halfsie outsider.

"Leave us out of it!" cried one.

"We've been through enough!" complained another.

"You should be grateful enough that we let that Pearlie girl escape with us!" yelled a third.

They all started shouting at once, until the three friends could no longer make out any individual voices, but instead experienced the sound they made as a kind of raging thunder, driven by all their shared pain and loss.

This was almost more than Fernie What could bear. They weren't hateful. They had lost almost everything they had to the war with Lord Obsidian and were all so wrapped up in their own hurt that they could offer nothing but anger at the suggestion that they go back and risk losing more. But they weren't hateful. It was the kind of anger that sounded more like pleas for mercy from beings who had already sacrificed more than they could afford to give.

Gustav stood there quietly, a pale little boy in a little black suit, momentarily driven to silence by all the rage around him.

Then the shouting died down a little and, as inevitably happens, somebody in the angry mob said one thing too much.

It was the high, reedy voice again. "We'd have to be *crazy* to go back there!"

Gustav suddenly stood straighter, emboldened

by the opportunity he'd just been handed. "Of *course* you would."

The response to that was a sudden pause that would have been a mass intake of breath had the crowd been composed of creatures who needed to breathe.

Gustav shouted, "I agree! You'd have to be *insane* to go back where a war's going on, even if that war has cost you everything. I agree! You'd have to have *lost all your common sense* just to go back where it's dangerous, even if you can make a difference there. I agree! You'd have to be *brainless morons* to go anywhere but where you're headed, even if there's nothing out there worth heading for."

Fernie reached for his arm. "Gustav—"

But he pulled away and finished saying what he had to say. "I know that what Lord Obsidian promises you is death, and worse than death! So, yes, you're all better off going however far you have to go to get away from the danger. Yes! You're all better off sitting down in some terrible empty place and waiting for things to get better. And, yes! Even if things don't ever get any better and you wind up staying out there forever, you're all better off always having the satisfaction of being able to look back on this one moment and remember that when your world was in trouble and you needed to decide what to do, you did the only *sensible* thing!"

The mob of shadows had fallen completely silent now. Many had stopped trudging along and stood still, arms at their sides, gaping at Gustav as if he were some species of strange animal.

Gustav lowered his voice to just above a whisper, but there was no doubt that thousands of shadows heard it. "As for me, when I look back at this moment, I'm going to remember that when I was given the chance to do something crazy, I *took* it."

He allowed the terrible weight of his words to hang in the air like a shroud. And then he turned on his heel and strode away from them.

As he passed between Fernie and Pearlie, he muttered, "Don't look back. We'll lose anybody following us if we show any doubt."

Not looking back was one of the most difficult things Fernie had ever done. It reminded her of an old story in one of her books, the tale of a grieving man named Orpheus who had been granted permission to bring his beloved wife,

Eurydice, back from the land of the dead. The only catch, Orpheus was told, was that she'd walk behind him and that he must never look back to make sure she was following; if he did, the land of the dead would own her forever. The poor man resisted temptation until he was well within sight of home . . . at which point he allowed himself a brief glance and saw his wife fade away, forever lost to him.

As a little girl of eight reading that famous tale for the first time, Fernie had felt nothing but scorn for Orpheus. *What an idiot,* she'd thought. He'd been told the rules and had only needed to follow them in order to have his wife back. Instead, he'd been as impatient as a kid at a birthday party, so eager to open his presents that he breaks the rules about waiting until after everybody was served cake, rips open the gifts prematurely, and is punished by having all of his lovely toys taken away for good. Young Fernie had told herself that if she was ever in a situation like that, she'd be much better at resisting temptation than that stupid old Orpheus had been.

But she'd been a foolish, overconfident little brat of eight then. As a wise ten-year-old who'd fought monsters and bad men and now found herself in a different situation where she had to avoid looking back, she felt a lot sorrier for Orpheus than she once had. This keeping-her-eyes-on-the-road-ahead stuff really wasn't very easy at all.

Eventually, though, she was able to draw up alongside Gustav and mutter, "You know, I've noticed that for a boy who never really knew any other people until he met us, you're awfully well practiced at giving speeches."

"I read a lot," Gustav said.

"I know. So do I. And?"

"So, if you read a lot of adventure stories in particular, you run into lots and lots of long-winded heroes making great glorious speeches to rally the troops or frighten off the bad guys. Those are always some of my favorite parts. From time to time I practice reading those speeches out loud, just to hear if the words sound anywhere near as impressive coming out of my own mouth. For instance," he said, apparently remembering one he particularly enjoyed, "did you ever hear of the English king Henry Vee?"

Fernie had never heard of any king named Henry Vee. "Sorry, no."

Gustav could only shake his head in awed admiration. "Too bad. That guy really knew how to talk."

Pearlie caught up to Gustav's other shoulder. "What about what you told them? That even trying to save our dads is crazy?"

"I meant that," said Gustav. "It's nuts. It's buggy. It's absolutely insane. We're outnumbered a billion to one, and we're heading into a country we don't know, without even a map or a plan. Even if we do find your father, let alone mine, we have no way of getting home unless we find some way to signal Lemuel's shadow aboard the Carousel."

Pearlie blinked. "Who's Lemuel and what's the Carousel and how would he go about rescuing us with it?"

"Sorry, Pearlie. That's all stuff you missed. I guess we have to catch you up just like you had to catch us up. But the whole point of everything I've been saying is something my grandpa wrote about in one of his books—that it's always the sensible people who tell you what can't be done and the crazy people, overall, who see that it has to be done and therefore do it anyway."

Pearlie seemed a little dizzied by this

conversation. "I guess the real difference is, we don't want to blindly jump off any cliffs or anything."

"Oh, I did that a few days ago," Gustav said seriously, "and it turned out to be one of those crazy ideas that worked out just fine."

Fernie happened to be looking at Pearlie when Gustav said this and saw a familiar look on her older sister's face. It was the same look she had often felt on her own face when Gustav dropped something inexplicable into a conversation. Being a little sister, a job that requires scoring as many points as possible, she took a little evil pleasure in rubbing it in. "Yes, Gustav. Jumping off that cliff really *was* the best way for us to get away from the giant spider."

Pearlie blinked some more. "Okay. I think I need to hear about the giant spider."

CHAPTER FOUR
LORD OBSIDIAN SEEMS TO HAVE
AN INFLATED OPINION OF HIMSELF

Up ahead, the gray slope rose toward a gray sky, with only the slightest difference in shade rendering it possible to tell the difference between one and the other. Wisps of shadow-stuff, yet another shade of gray, overflowed the gaps between those peaks and came apart high above, becoming part of the featureless cloud cover. It was such a bleak sight, all but eliminating any hope of anything good on the other side of those mountains, that Fernie shuddered even as she set her jaw and concentrated on telling Pearlie the story of the past few days, which included that giant spider.

She finally got to the point where she and Gustav instructed Lemuel Gloom's shadow to keep the Cryptic Carousel in flight over the Dark Country and await the signal that it was time to come down and save them.

With a quick glance at Gustav, who was scouting up ahead, Pearlie repeated, "A signal? What kind of signal?"

"Gustav didn't say."

"He didn't?"

"No."

"Isn't the whole point of a signal that it's something you arrange in advance so the person you're trying to signal knows what to watch out for?"

"Usually," said Fernie. "But Gustav wasn't really sure what we'd run into in the Dark Country or what kind of signal he'd be able to send. So he just told Lemuel's shadow to watch for something big."

Pearlie chewed on this for several seconds, as if it were a piece of stringy meat she couldn't swallow. "I don't know, Fernie. I don't think signals work that way. I mean, suppose Dad drops me off at the mall and I promise to let him know when I want to be picked back up. I can promise to send him a text . . . or I can say I'll send whatever random signal I can come up with at the spur of the moment, in which case he's at home waiting for a call and I'm making a fool of myself standing in the food court for an hour, waving a napkin like a flag."

Fernie had to think about that. "Dad would probably still come."

"Yes, but that's because he's *Dad*. He probably followed me in and spent the whole day waiting for me in the food court."

"True. The second you started waving the napkin, he'd be *right there*."

"The point," Pearlie said doggedly, "is that Gustav's made no plans for what the signal's going to be. He doesn't know for sure that he can send a signal Lemuel's shadow can see from the air. He just assumes he can. I'm not sure that's smart."

"It's smart," said Fernie, even if Pearlie had managed to plant a little seed of doubt in her mind.

Then the slope grew steep, and the girls needed to save their breath.

To the left, a massive parade of refugees continued to flow on the well-worn path down the mountain. They had nothing to say as the halfsie boy and the two human girls walked alongside them. Most just looked at their feet— or at the clouds of flowing, shadowy mist that obscured the places where their feet would have been. Fernie's heart broke for them. It was downright infuriating to remember how much was being taken from so many, just to fuel the dreams of the madman who had begun life as a crackpot writer named Howard Philip October.

The oddest thing about the mountain itself was that there was no grit to it. There should have been. Every other big rock or pile of rocks she'd ever seen had spent years and years being exposed to wind and rain and had places where the stone had worn down to dirt or where it was covered with a layer of dust loose enough to come off in her hands. Some of the big ones were so crumbly, it was dangerous to get close to them because of falling stones. This wasn't just true of rock piles or cliffs, but also of brick walls. She'd never seen a brick wall, even a brand-new one, that wasn't already eager to give up a few little brick pebbles. This was the nature of rock. It crumbled.

This mountain was nothing like that. It was as solid and smooth as polished marble, completely free of dust or grit, even though the ledges and outcroppings and even little crevices all looked the same way they would have if they'd formed their shapes by being hammered by wind or rain. It just didn't feel real, the way one of the imperfect, stony, dusty mountains back home would have. It felt less like a mountain and more like something a giant sculptor had made of some unbreakable material and put in place at the beginning of time, confident that it would last until time's end.

Up ahead, Gustav reached the summit and stood there, hands on hips, catching his breath as he surveyed the view. His black suit was very easy to see against the gray sky. "Now *this* is interesting," he said.

Fernie had learned to dread Gustav's idea of interesting. "What?"

"Lord Obsidian seems to have a pretty inflated opinion of himself."

Fernie wouldn't have normally considered Lord Obsidian's inflated opinion of himself remarkable enough to be worth mentioning. She couldn't imagine anybody calling himself *Lord* anything if he hadn't already decided that he was a pretty special guy. Just calling yourself *Lord* meant that you'd given up on shyness, insecurity, humility, and a reasonable sense of perspective.

But whatever Gustav had seen seemed to

impress him enough for him to make a special point of it, so she scrambled up the last few feet of slope and joined him on the ridge overlooking the Dark Country.

As soon as she saw what he saw, she said, "Oh."

The "oh" had very little to do with Lord Obsidian, though.

It had more to do with the Dark Country itself, which from this angle resembled nothing so much as a sea of rolling gray clouds so vast that she could not make out its other side. It was like standing on a cliff overlooking the ocean and trying to make out some beach thousands of miles away. Appreciating that another continent was out there somewhere and understanding that ships had been known to cross from here to there and back was not the same thing as feeling happy about the prospect of trying to cross that distance by swimming.

The ring of mountains that completely surrounded the beclouded land stretched away to Fernie's left and right. She got the impression that, somewhere far away through all that darkness, the other side of the Dark Country was marked by more mountains just like the one where she stood. But the line of mountains on either side of her extended as far away as she could see, and that line only seemed to curve a little bit before it disappeared into the horizon.

Fernie's voice sounded awfully tiny to her own ears. "It's . . . big."

Gustav seemed wholly unconcerned. "Yup."

"Really big," she said, as if he hadn't gotten the point.

"I know. It's a big place. Big as the Earth. From what I hear, it has hills and plains and deserts and swamps and jungles and entire oceans, not to mention some cold places where nothing can live and some wild places with vicious hungry animals as big as houses."

She still had to believe he hadn't gotten the point. "But you can't find one lost man in a place as big as the Earth!"

"No, normally you can't . . . but then it would normally be just as hard to find one *girl*, and we weren't here for even five minutes before we ran into Pearlie. That's a crazy coincidence. But maybe luck's on our side."

Behind them, Pearlie said, "I haven't had a chance to tell you how I managed to join the refugees."

"I noticed," Gustav admitted, "and I suspect it's a good story. But that's not what I'm trying to point out to the two of you now. Over there? Sticking up out of the clouds in that direction? Look closely."

He pointed, but for Fernie it was a little bit like standing on the top of the tallest building in a city and having a friend try to point out one little two-story house several neighborhoods away.

"I don't see what you're pointing at," Fernie confessed.

Pearlie put her hands on the sides of Fernie's face and adjusted the angle of her head. "Once you see it you won't be able to stop seeing it. Look."

Fernie looked . . . and after a few seconds spotted something that made her heart thump in her chest: an ugly little face peering at her from out of churning clouds an unimaginable distance away.

It was the long and narrow face of an intelligent, bookish man with a hawk nose, a high forehead, and a massive jaw: a face that only barely resembled one worn by a deadly monster called the shadow eater, who had once chased Fernie and Gustav around the Gloom house.

The shadow eater's face had been a loose-fitting, lumpy sack of flesh, shifting and bulging in odd places from all the shadows trapped and moving around inside him, the same way a pillowcase would shift and bulge if somebody decided to fill it with spiders and worms. But the Shadow Eater had worn the man's face when it was just an empty sack of skin. The face emerging from the clouds was younger, more chiseled, and what that face looked like while it was still being worn by a human being.

"Gustav! That's Howard Philip October!"

"No, it's not," said Gustav, who was nothing if not literal-minded. "That's just the head of a giant *statue* of Howard Philip October."

It was indeed a giant carved figure of the strange and demented writer who had harassed Gustav's grandfather Lemuel, arranged the death of the woman who would have been Gustav's mother, taken Gustav's father away, and ultimately become the conquering despot known as Lord Obsidian, at which point his villainy had ceased to be a hobby and become a full-time job.

Fernie was impressed despite herself. "That thing's got to be *huge*."

"Bigger than it has any right to be," Gustav said, "since it's got to be a few hundred miles away."

It wasn't easy to judge distances over the clouds, because there were no closer objects Fernie could use for comparison. Fernie had based her own estimate of the head's current distance on her own understanding of what was and wasn't possible, which was always a risky thing to do when dealing with matters involving the world of shadows. Gustav's own guess, which she knew at once to be more accurate than hers, made her head feel about to explode from ideas too large for her to easily imagine.

Gustav went on. "The head alone must be the size of a small mountain range, and since I can also make out a neck and a pair of shoulders beneath it, there must be a whole standing body there, just tall enough for only the head to emerge above the clouds."

Fernie's head felt as fluttery as a jar filled with playful butterflies. "That's not just huge. That's . . . you know . . ."

Fernie had a decent vocabulary for a girl her age, but couldn't come up with a word more expressive than *huge*.

Pearlie placed a protective hand on her shoulder. "*Huge* works."

"Why would *anybody* need a statue of himself that huge?"

"I wouldn't," said Gustav. "I don't need any statues of myself, big or small. I know what I look like."

Fernie stared at the giant October head and tried to figure out some way to avoid being frightened of a power great enough to even consider building such a thing. For long seconds nothing occurred to her.

Forgetting her father's plight for a moment, she came very close to chickening out. Maybe this adventure was more than they could handle. Maybe they shouldn't go on at all. Maybe it would be smarter to back down and make their way home to Sunnyside Terrace.

And then she realized something that allowed her to look at the faraway face and derive some genuine hope from it. "Gustav? It's . . . awfully sad, isn't it?"

"That's what I was thinking," Gustav replied.

A truly big man wouldn't have needed a giant statue of himself. The statue in the clouds would have been needed by somebody who felt tiny all the time . . . by a person who blustered and bullied and ran around trying to conquer things but, deep inside, knew he wasn't all that much.

This didn't mean he wasn't dangerous. If anything, it might have made him more dangerous. There's nothing more dangerous, in any world, than a tiny person willing to hurt other people in order to prove that he's bigger than he really is. But Fernie was unable to look at the giant head without knowing that, on some level, she'd never take Lord Obsidian seriously ever again.

Pearlie seemed to feel the same way, because she chose that moment to laugh out loud. It was a welcome sound, but also a profoundly unexpected one, given how quiet she'd been since the Dark Country came into view. She hugged her stomach as if to hold herself together while hilarity made her sink to her knees.

For one ghastly moment, Fernie thought Pearlie was not laughing, but sobbing. "Are you okay?"

Pearlie indicated with a hand wave that she was fine. Even then it took her several seconds to catch her breath enough to say, "Wow. I needed that."

"What?" asked Fernie.

"That's a really, really, *really* big statue."

"So?"

"So I found myself wondering who has to clean it up if the Dark Country has any really, really, *really* big pigeons."

One stunned moment of silence later, Fernie started laughing, too.

Every once in a while, life provides a laugh that won't go away, because it keeps being rekindled every time you look at the face of the person laughing with you. Sometimes even the one person in the group who doesn't laugh at all (in this case, Gustav) strikes you as equally hilarious because he's so serious about whatever you're laughing at. The two girls needed several minutes to stop, and they had just managed to get themselves back under control, their bellies hurting, when Gustav unwittingly said the one thing designed to start them up again.

He said, "I don't get it."

Well, *of course* he didn't get it. He'd never been to a public park. He'd seen statues, but all of his were indoors. His front yard had ravens who said "caw," but it was possible that he'd never actually seen a pigeon or had any idea what they did to statues. This was all pretty sad, really, maybe even as sad in its own way as Lord Obsidian's wan attempt to compensate for a poor self-image. But there was something about Gustav's total incomprehension at the sight of two close sisters reduced to breathless giggles that somehow made the hilarity funny all over again. It became funnier still when both Fernie and Pearlie kept meeting those serious eyes and couldn't gather up enough breath to explain the joke.

This went on for so long that Gustav finally said, "If he could see the two of you right now, he'd probably be surrendering already."

CHAPTER FIVE
THE RETURN OF SOMEBODY REMARKABLY UNPLEASANT

Unfortunately, that was the last laugh any of them had for a while.

They discussed what to do next, and Gustav said it made little sense to use the reverse route the shadow refugees had used. After all, that would just lead straight to the horrors the refugees had been fleeing, horrors Gustav could see from this height and which he described as the advance of a shadow army that was better off avoided.

This made sense to the girls, but without hunger, thirst, the need for sleep, or the rising and setting of the sun, it was impossible to tell for sure how many hours or days they spent wandering the mountaintops without Gustav declaring any particular spot a suitable way down. The result was a deadly dull, exhausting, and dangerous slog. Unlike the number of hikes

Mrs. What had taken the girls on across other mountain trails, this journey wasn't even kind enough to reward their efforts with a beautiful view. Here, the only views available were a bunch of gray clouds on one side and an endless dull emptiness on the other.

There was nothing to do but talk or remain silent, and neither was very satisfying.

At one point, Pearlie muttered a sarcastic, "I'm almost sorry I didn't bring a camera."

Fernie looked out upon the nothing, surrounded by nothing, on top of nothing, capped by nothing, and said, "I agree! You could have made a postcard of it!"

"It would have been a very mean postcard," Pearlie said seriously. "I mean, what do you write on postcards, anyway? *Wish you were here*, right? Considering where we are, that would be a really stinky thing to say to someone. You would only send it to someone you didn't like."

"I don't even have Mrs. Everwiner's address," Fernie concluded.

This was the least fun of Fernie's adventures with Gustav so far, because even while they'd been running from the Beast or fighting the People Taker or hiding from the shadow eater or being scared by Hieronymus Spector or being chased by the Four Terrors or trying not to get eaten by Silverspinner, they had never been bored. There had always been something happening, something that gave her something to think about. Now, it was only with a tremendous act of will that Fernie managed to resist asking the mostly silent Gustav if they were 'there yet,' wherever 'there' happened to be.

Eventually, though, Gustav stopped, gazed down into the Dark Country upon a patch of rolling gray clouds that to Fernie's eyes looked just like any other patch of rolling gray clouds they'd looked down upon before, and uttered a deeply satisfied, "All right, then. Here we go."

Fernie saw nothing about the view from this mountaintop that struck her as in any way different from the views of every other mountaintop they had passed. Even the angle of the giant Howard Philip October head didn't seem to have changed all that much. The likely distance they would have had to walk around the mountains before being able to see that distant monument in profile, let alone from the back, was greater than she could even begin to imagine. And yet she could see from the set of Gustav's jaw that he really did seem to be satisfied. "Why? What do you see?" she asked him.

"Nothing," said Gustav.

She protested, "But that's all we've been seeing all along!"

"That may be all *you've* been seeing, but it's not all *I've* been seeing."

"What have you been seeing?"

"Oh, well . . . Back when we first reached the top, I saw a whole bunch of shadow cities crumbling to dust as Lord Obsidian's armies swept through them. Not long after that, I saw a dense forest of spiny plants that would have cut us to ribbons if we'd tried to walk among them. Then I saw a place where the ground was all covered with terrible grasping hands that probably would have seized us if we'd tried to pass. After that, there was a gooey marsh, and we might have been able to trudge through that, but it would have been very difficult and very messy, and I didn't like the look of the flies."

"You can see flies from all the way up here?"

"Not normal flies, no. But I saw these."

"What was so visible about these flies?"

"I think you assumed I meant *small* flies."

"And these—"

"You could have put seats on the back of the smaller ones and used them as school buses."

She shuddered. "Okay. Good place to skip."

"After that, there was nothing much in particular, a village or two, but none of them looked friendly enough to be worth going to, especially with all those billboards saying things like *No Trespassers* and *Go Away* and *Warning: Anybody We Don't Like Will Be Fed to the Gnarfle.*"

Pearlie beat her sister to the obvious question. "What's a gnarfle?"

"I don't have even the slightest idea," Gustav confessed, "but I think the important message to take away from that sign is that we don't want to be fed to it."

This struck both sisters as sensible.

Fernie rubbed her nose. "And now you say you're seeing nothing?"

"Pretty much. Just one of those places that are considered too distant and out-of-the-way and unpleasant for anybody to bother living in. I don't see any armies fighting over it, any traffic crossing it, or any obstacles that we won't be able to pass. Just . . . like, I said, nothing. Or almost nothing. And nothing's *good* in the Dark Country."

A dark voice behind them exclaimed, "Ha! *Nothing's* good in the Dark Country."

All this time, Fernie had obeyed the don't-look-back advice as she'd become so focused on the road ahead that she'd forgotten all about it. Now, as she and the others turned, she saw a small group of shadows gathered so close to one another that their gray substance overlapped and seemed to flow from one figure to the next.

The gravelly voice of the shadow who'd spoken up struck her as strangely familiar, but right now she found herself more concerned with the odd way he'd repeated Gustav's words. He'd made a point of emphasizing the word *nothing* differently than Gustav had.

Fernie asked him, "What's your point?"

The shadow chuckled nastily. "It all depends on what word you emphasize. When the stupid boy said that nothing's *good* in the Dark Country, he meant it in the sense that the empty places here are better than those filled with dangers. When I replied that *nothing's* good in the Dark Country, I meant to say that you won't find any places that fit such a stupid, limited description of good. The Dark Country isn't safe for flesh-and-blood people. It's one of the few things I like about the wretched place."

Pearlie said something surprising then. "Yes. You kept saying that."

Fernie stared at her sister. "You know this guy?"

"Yes, she does," the gravelly voiced shadow said. "And yet here she is, proving what an idiot she is by marching back in, no matter how hard it was for me to get her out to begin with. It makes saving her in the first place even more of a waste of time than I thought."

He stepped forward, radiating the open resentment of an unpleasant neighbor upset that some kids down the street might be having fun he couldn't ruin. He took the form of an old man in a dirty undershirt and baggy shorts, with unpleasant eyes half-hidden behind scraggly eyebrows.

Fernie finally remembered where she'd heard that unpleasant voice just as his face grew distinct enough to be recognized. "Cousin Cyrus!"

Pearlie glanced at her in sudden surprise. "You know Cousin Cyrus, too?"

"Not well," Fernie said, remembering their one prior meeting.

Back at the house, Gustav had invoked an old debt to force the cantankerous and antisocial shadow to take news of Pearlie's kidnapping to Great-Aunt Mellifluous in the Dark Country. The revelation that Pearlie must have run into Cousin Cyrus at some later point was just the latest thing in this adventure to confuse Fernie What. She asked him directly, "She knows you?"

"Of course she knows me," Cousin Cyrus snapped. "And I have the deep displeasure of knowing her, too. I had to *spend time* with her, answering her foolish questions until I was ready to tear my hair out."

Fernie glanced at Gustav. "I never knew shadow hair could be torn out."

"That one's even news to me," Gustav confessed. He cast a curious gaze at Pearlie and asked, "Where did you meet Cousin Cyrus?"

"In the Dark Country, after Dad was captured by the minions. I was just wandering around lost, feeling doomed, when he showed up to help me."

This made even less sense to Fernie, as the one thing she had picked up about Cousin

Cyrus was that he never did favors for anybody unless he was forced to. "But why would *he* help you?"

Cousin Cyrus snarled. "Because that annoying old woman Great-Aunt Mellifluous made me, that's why! The intolerable halfsie boy invoked the last of my debts to him just to get me to take her the message that your silly sister and idiot father were in trouble, but just when I thought I was done with that errand, she turned out to be too busy planning an important mission behind enemy lines to get involved herself, and she invoked one of my many debts to *her* to make me find this stupid girl and get her out of the Dark Country. I arrived on the scene too late to save your father, which was fine as far as I was concerned—less work for me—but this stupid girl was still around, and I still had to endure all her mewling and whining for as long as it took me to dump her with the refugees and satisfy myself that she was safe."

Fernie looked at her sister. "Mewling and whining doesn't sound like you at all."

"It wasn't," Pearlie replied. "He insulted me so much that after a while I stopped being scared and started insulting him right back."

"Liar!" Cousin Cyrus shouted. "You whined nonstop! Don't say you didn't!"

"Maybe a little," Pearlie said, admitting the horrible truth.

"Either way," Gustav told Cousin Cyrus, "if you fulfilled your obligation to Great-Aunt Mellifluous, why are you following us now?"

"It's not because I have a choice, boy. Once I got rid of the stupid girl, I was looking forward to going back to the house and curling up in my favorite pile of dust. But Mellifluous's spies intercepted me at once and told me, 'It's not that easy, you old fool, your debt's not repaid yet! You can't just leave Pearlie in the wastelands! You have to stay with her in case she needs help again!' So I returned to the silly girl and walked ten paces behind her wherever she went."

Pearlie said, "You never let me know you'd come back."

"Nobody ever said I had to let you know I was watching over you or endure your witless questions again. That I've spared myself while we've spent all this time hiking up and down hills."

There was a moment of silence until Pearlie sighed. "This really isn't fair. In the fairy tales, the damsel in distress always gets rescued by a *nice* person."

"Don't worry," said Gustav. "I'm a nice person, and I'm still working on it." He looked past the glowering Cousin Cyrus at the half dozen more indistinct shadows gathered behind him and said, "And the rest of you? Are you the only refugees who agreed to join us?"

For a moment, the only response was a soft murmur from the crowd that failed to involve any actual words. Maybe they were shy. Maybe they'd never been around solid people of any kind and were unsure about the best way to talk to them. Maybe they were just interested in a good show.

Then one, wearing the form of a delicately beautiful woman with soft cheeks and wide eyes and pale gray hair that billowed around her face like clouds, advanced and spoke in an ethereal voice, with the slightest trace of an accent Fernie didn't recognize. "My name is Anemone."

"It's good to meet you, Anemone. We appreciate your joining us."

Anemone shook her pretty head. "You haven't shown us you're worth joining."

"We've come this far," Gustav pointed out.

The answer to that was gentle laughter. "You have only succeeded in walking into danger, not out of it."

"So?"

"So there's a fable among our kind of a mountain goat from your world who tried to leap from one crag to another, but instead fell into a bottomless valley. On every ledge he passed on the way down, he saw others of his kind watching his plunge. He called out to them, saying, 'Why not follow me? This is easy! After all, I've come this far!' You see, he thought that was an admirable accomplishment. He didn't know that the true test of his ability to survive would be the ground."

"He sounds like a pretty stupid goat," Fernie declared.

"Indeed. That is the very point. But in traveling as far as you have, you three may be no smarter. It is clear to us that you know nothing of the perils that still await you. We know that you will blunder into them, regardless of where you choose to enter the Dark Country. We're willing to follow you to see if you possess the qualities you will need to survive them, let alone find and confront Lord Obsidian. But we'll have to see more before we offer any assistance or make any promises."

Fernie wasn't at all happy with that. She came close to telling Anemone that she and her companions weren't welcome if all they were willing to do was follow around at a respectful distance without ever trying to be useful.

But Gustav regarded the remaining five shadows, considering what help they might be able to provide at some later point. He didn't offer them another stirring speech. He just nodded and said, "All right. You can follow us until you make up your minds. But I'd appreciate names for the rest of you, if any of you have them."

Only two of the remaining five shadows admitted to having names. One, a robed figure whose face remained indistinct except for a white dot that seemed to be the tip of a very long nose emerging from the darkness of his otherwise all-concealing hood called himself Caliban, and added that he strongly doubted that Gustav and his companions would survive in the Dark Country for more than five minutes. "I believe you are a waste of my time," he concluded. "But I am willing to be proved wrong."

The other, a dark-eyed, straggly haired and bearded fellow bearing a shadow sword and wearing a helmet equipped with two long horns that curved together like parentheses, introduced himself as the shadow of an ancient warrior known to friends and enemies alike as Olaf Who Smells So Awful That He Can Make Invading Enemy Armies Collapse in Stunned Amazement. Advising Gustav and his friends to call him Olaf for short, the shadow went on to explain, "My human wasn't the most talented swordsman who ever lived, but he didn't have to be. He really did smell as awful as advertised, and by the time he got close to any enemy, most of them were too busy curled on the ground being sick to fight back. As a result, his tribe never lost a battle. Unlike these others, I've already made up my mind to fight on your side, but unfortunately, I won't be as formidable as he was, as I only wear the real Olaf's shape and not his powerful odor."

"That's okay," Pearlie said. "Honestly."

The remaining three shadows, vague outlines who could not even be distinguished as male or female, explained that they'd never been the shadows of any human beings and had never seen the point of ever developing any human personalities. They didn't have opinions, either, which is why, like Anemone and Caliban, they were just waiting to see how Gustav and the girls fared before making a decision on whether to help.

Gustav didn't seem disappointed or surprised to find their shadow companions offering such an ambivalent show of support. "Would you object to answering a question from time to time? Like, for instance, what you know of this spot, below us?"

"It is called the Rarely," Anemone replied, "among other reasons because it is rarely visited and rarely thought about and rarely worth the trouble of crossing."

"Which means that it probably isn't being guarded," mused Gustav. "Is it safe?"

The shadow woman cocked her head. "Rarely."

Gustav seemed to have expected that, because he nodded, turned away from her and, after a long silent look at Cousin Cyrus that communicated nothing Fernie was able to see, told the girls, "All I can tell you is that I don't see any immediate dangers down there, and that there's a small light burning a few miles away that might or might not be friendly. We might be able to pick up some information there. At the very least, it's something to head for."

Fernie remembered to be frightened and then promptly did her best to forget it again. "Might as well get on with it, I guess."

"Pearlie?"

Pearlie was even less enthusiastic about it. "Why not? I don't have any other plans for the afternoon."

Gustav nodded, then turned toward the Dark Country and started his descent into the endless bubbling layer of shadow-stuff just a short walk down the slope.

The girls found it a difficult walk, but not for the same reason walks are usually described as difficult. The slope wasn't too steep, the ground wasn't too slippery, and there weren't any loose stones or protruding roots to send them tumbling down the mountainside like that other girl from the silly nursery rhyme whose family had been shortsighted enough to place its only well on the top of a hill. (Fernie hadn't even gone to nursery school before she first started finding that rhyme ridiculous, in part because she was a smart girl and knew that nobody ever digs a well on the top of a hill.)

The girls found the descent difficult only because there was something about the churning sea of shadow-stuff before them and the way it hid everything else beneath it from view that gave their legs an argumentative personality of their own and made it necessary to win a debate with them, at the rate of once every step or so. *No,* Fernie's legs kept saying, *you really don't want to go where you're making us go. Yes,* Fernie kept silently telling them, *I do. No,* her legs kept insisting, *we think you haven't thought this all the way through. No,* she had to answer, *I think I have.*

Nothing, though, was quite as loud about its disapproval of the destination ahead as her stomach, which seemed to perform somersaults of angry protest. It acted like it wanted to leap out of her mouth and scurry away into the distance, screaming, "Flee! Flee!" Fernie had missed being able to eat food in the more than a week she'd been relying on her own shadow, wherever it was, to keep her alive by eating for her, but when she considered how jumpy her belly was, she found herself grateful that there wasn't any real food in it. That was the last thing she needed.

The top of Gustav's head disappeared beneath the rolling clouds, and Fernie found her feet about to step into the same darkness.

Pearlie grabbed her hand and murmured, "I can't believe I'm going back there."

"Well," Fernie managed, in a voice so faint that calling it a whisper would have been giving it too much credit, "I can't believe you're going back there, either."

"It's got to be the dumbest thing either one of us has ever done," said Pearlie.

The mists swallowed them without even seeming to notice. The shadow companions followed the girls and were also swallowed. The mountaintop the friends had abandoned went back to being what it had been before their arrival: a high, silent, lonely place in the sky, unaffected by any of the desperate battles fought by any who traveled far below.

CHAPTER SIX
OLAF AND COUSIN CYRUS DON'T LIKE EACH OTHER VERY MUCH

"I thought it would be dark," said Fernie.

"It is dark," replied Gustav.

"I mean, too dark to see, like in a closet with the door closed, or a house when the neighborhood's blacked out. I expected to be tripping around like a blind person without a flashlight."

"Blind people don't use flashlights," Pearlie pointed out.

Fernie had heard the silly thing she'd just said even as it left her mouth. "You know what I mean."

"Yes, I do," Pearlie agreed. "And blind people still don't use flashlights."

"*Whatever.* The point is, I thought it would be dark, and it's not dark. It's just kind of . . . dreary."

It was indeed. Upon passing the top layer

of mist, Fernie had indeed seen nothing but impenetrable blackness all around her, and had spent a few seconds worrying that she'd have to turn back and get no closer to her imperiled father than she was already. But then the darkness seemed to lift, she started to be able to pick out shapes, and the details filled in. What she saw now was a gray valley, extending as far as her eyes could see, with differently shaded patches all crowded together in the far distance. There wasn't a single patch of bright color anywhere; even her own sister's hair, a brilliant red most of the time, had gone pale and dreary, as if all the life had been removed and nothing but the vague suggestion of color had been put back in.

Although the misty shadow-stuff that submerged them could now be seen through, thicker tendrils of it sometimes drifted by, like patches of dye that hadn't been properly mixed with the rest of the formula. She was able to see quite far even so, even to the immense, impossibly tall legs of the Howard Philip October statue, towering over the landscape an unthinkable distance away. As horizons went, it was so far away that she didn't think even a lifetime of walking would be enough to get her there. It would take a long time, she felt, just to get to that one bright spot Gustav had mentioned.

Everything close to her looked empty, drained of color and of life. But it didn't seem to be pitch-black, as she'd expected.

Gustav said, "You're wrong. It's too dark to see."

"But I *can* see."

"You could see in my house, too, even in the places that would have been far too dark for you if you were depending on light alone. You could see even in the places where there was no light at all. That's because it's not just your eyes seeing everything you're looking at. It's also your head."

"Huh?"

"It's one of the more helpful things about shadow-magic. Have you ever been in a dark place, where you really couldn't see anything, for a long time? Like, for an hour or more?"

Fernie remembered an infamous game of hide-and-seek from very early in her childhood when she had huddled in a wardrobe in the back of a closet, thinking that she was doing really well. At the same time, unknown to her, Pearlie had forgotten all about the game and had gone into the basement to play with plastic dinosaurs. Fernie had waited so long that she'd grown bored and then tired and had finally curled up into a deep nap, completely missing her sister's tears, her mother's calls, and her father's vocal fretting until her family was about to report her missing to the police. "Yes."

"Well, while you were in that darkness, didn't you start to see shapes? Faces? Little bursts of light that weren't there? That was shadow-magic trying to work inside your head to help you see. It didn't work very well because all it had to work with was the weak, watery darkness people encounter in the world you know. What you walked through in my house, and what we're walking through now, is darkness of an entirely different kind—darkness so dark that it's not just the absence of light but the exact *opposite* of light, which is something few people have experienced. Wait until we get deeper into the Dark Country. From what I hear, there are places so dark that they feel almost *bright*."

He turned around and again started to lead them forward. But then he pivoted on his left ankle, swung his right leg around like a crane seeking a fresh weight to lift, and returned to the girls. His habitual frown now bore the stamp of sudden worry. "Excuse me. Did one of you just cackle evilly to yourself?"

Fernie hadn't heard anything. "Not me."

Gustav frowned. "You're right. I've heard you laugh a bunch of times, and it didn't sound one bit like any of yours."

Pearlie said, "It wasn't one of mine, either."

"No, it wouldn't be. This didn't sound like a girl laugh at all. It sounded like a nasty, bitter, cruel, evil-old-man laugh." He peered over the heads of the girls at the handful of shadows following them, and in particular at Cousin Cyrus, who was peering at his own feet in the manner of a poor student hoping the teacher wouldn't call on him in class. "Cousin Cyrus? That was you, wasn't it?"

Cousin Cyrus tried to avoid his eyes, but soon seemed to realize he couldn't manage that trick forever and glared back in contempt. "I didn't cackle evilly."

"It sounded just like one of yours."

The elderly shadow scratched his shoulder, and then his rump, and then the small sliver of belly that his dirty undershirt failed to cover.

"Wasn't me." He pointed at Olaf. "It was him."

"Liar!" cried Olaf.

Gustav glared at Cousin Cyrus. "Should I believe you?"

"I don't give one good loud fart whether you believe me or not. I don't owe you any dang explanations."

"No," Gustav agreed. "If you were anybody else, you wouldn't. But I *know* you, Cyrus. You hate everybody. I can't imagine your cackling at anything but a terrible secret."

Cousin Cyrus lowered his big scraggly eyebrows enough to hide both of the cold and unpleasant eyes behind them. "It was him. But this is going to be one long and tedious trip if you're going to insist on stopping to blame me for every stupid random noise."

Gustav studied him for a long time, spared the briefest of glances for the handful of other shadows trailing close behind, and then shrugged it off before once again turning his attention back to their descent.

As they reached the bottom of the mountain and with it the land known as the Rarely, the path widened and they were able to spread out a little, Gustav scouting up ahead and the two girls keeping each other company about twenty steps behind him. They didn't have to walk far before Fernie found herself able to spot the burning light Gustav had mentioned. It flickered, like a distant star, and seemed as forlorn and out of place in all the darkness surrounding it as a fish would be in the center of an empty grocery store parking lot. Fernie didn't know whether whatever cast that light would turn out to be a good thing or a bad thing, but found that her eyes were so starved for real light of any kind that she could barely wait to draw near and take comfort from whatever it illuminated.

The hooded Caliban drifted close to the girls and said, "I must confess, you've survived a lot longer than I ever imagined."

"No thanks to you," Pearlie muttered.

The slightly brighter dot that was the tip of Caliban's nose bobbed in the impenetrable darkness under his hood. "If that was supposed to sting, I assure you that it failed. I can't feel guilty over failing to provide help when I have not yet promised to do so . . . and the dangers that still lie between you and the lair of Lord Obsidian are so great that the chances of your surviving much longer are, really, quite poor.

Still, I thought you'd appreciate the compliment, for what it's worth."

"It's not worth much," Fernie said, "but thanks all the same."

Cousin Cyrus drifted by on Fernie's other side, his weathered features curling into a nasty scowl. "You're wasting your time with the likes of her, Caliban. Her kind never appreciates what we do for them."

"That's not true," said Fernie. "I've made friends with my shadow. I *like* her."

"Mine's a little harder to know," Pearlie said, "but I've made friends with her, too."

"So you claim," Cousin Cyrus sneered, "and yet I note that neither of them seem to be anywhere around the immediate neighborhood. You ask me, I don't think they're lost. I think they just got sick and tired of you and abandoned you, the way I abandoned the mean old man whose shadow I was all those years ago."

Fernie said, "You know what I think?"

Cousin Cyrus grumbled, "I couldn't care less what you think."

Fernie told him anyway. "I think the only reason you're so mean and miserable all the time is that you think it's less work than being nice. You don't get anything out of it. It doesn't make you any happier. But you're too lazy to try anything else."

"That's where you're wrong," said Cousin Cyrus. "I'm mean and miserable because I don't find anything about other people that's worth the trouble of liking. I enjoy being mean and miserable. It's what I'm good at. Like you're good at being annoying."

Olaf hastened to catch up, swinging his shadow sword before him as if already battling monsters that only he could see. "Come, now! There's no need for us to snipe at one another like that. We're companions, embarking on a great adventure. We should be singing songs and trading tales of our past acts of derring-do."

"You don't have any past acts of derring-do," Cousin Cyrus snarled. "You're just the shadow of a person who did, and from what you say the only heroic thing about him was his stench."

Olaf's face fell. "True, but I was with him all that time, and I do remember some of the battle songs and all of the more interesting stories. What about you, dear Fernie? What songs do you know?"

The only song that came to Fernie's mind at

the moment had to do with a boy named Jimmy who cracked corn for some reason, an act that even the song admitted was not worth caring about. As for tales of past acts of derring-do, she'd accumulated a few since beginning her adventures with Gustav Gloom, but wasn't in any mood to share them at the moment. Still, Olaf did seem to be the only one of the party's shadow companions interested in making an honest effort to be both helpful and pleasant, so she answered politely, "Do you have any in mind?"

The shadow knight grinned happily, displaying teeth uneven enough to make his mouth look like one of those ancient cemeteries where all the tombstones are in danger of falling over. "Why, of course. When I traveled with my human, the warrior known far and wide for his unbearable stench, I saw him defend the bridge over the River Tepid! I helped him capture the Donut of Fate! I—"

But they were never to hear the no doubt amazing saga of the Donut of Fate, because that's when, ten steps up ahead, Gustav cried, "Everybody down!"

The two girls fell to the ground at once.

The shadows were slower to follow Gustav's direction, probably because none of them—not even Olaf—had yet agreed to take his orders. But after a moment of studying the landscape ahead for some clue to Gustav's reason for suddenly requiring stealth, they also sank to the gray earth and flattened to the thickness of area rugs, hugging the dirt as if trying to keep it warm.

Long seconds of silence later, Cousin Cyrus declared, "This is stupid."

"I disagree," said Olaf.

"That's because *you're* stupid," said Cousin Cyrus.

"And you're a cad and a bounder," Olaf retorted.

"I don't even know what those words mean, but I think I take offense anyway."

Anemone shushed them. "Be quiet, you. The young man's returning."

Gustav's pale white face bobbed like a glow-in-the-dark ball bouncing in a darkened room as he scrambled back on all fours to rejoin them. "It's a house."

"What's a house?" asked Olaf.

"That light up ahead. It's a house. And not a shadow house, either. It's an actual, solid, three-story house, complete with sloping roof and brick chimney. The light is a lantern burning in the window, and I saw a man—not the shadow of a man, but a real flesh-and-blood human being—walking around the front yard before he went back inside. It's all as out of place in the Dark Country as anything I can possibly imagine."

"What color is it painted?" asked Fernie.

Gustav blinked. "Why is *that* important?"

"I want to know."

"It's gray, of course, like everything else around here. Why?"

"Because if it were Fluorescent Salmon, I'd suspect a trap."

"Yes," Gustav agreed. "You're right. That *would* be a little too convenient."

Olaf peeled his flattened head from the dirt to glance from one face to the other in search of clues that might have clarified the conversation for him. "What kind of strange person has a Fluorescent Salmon house?"

Gustav ignored him. "Question is, do we want to avoid the house or do we risk knocking on the front door to see who the man is and if there's anything he can do to help us?"

Pearlie nibbled on a finger. "He could be working for Lord Obsidian."

"Yes. That is one of the things we'd be risking. Or he could be a bad guy for any number of other reasons. But he could also be an ally, and frankly . . ." Gustav hesitated, glanced at their shadow companions, then bit the bullet and said it: "No offense, but so far we're not doing as well as I'd hoped in the ally department. I think this is one of those decisions that need to be put up to a vote."

Anemone spoke for her fellow shadows. "Do we have votes?"

Fernie considered that outrageous. "Why would most of you get votes when you haven't agreed to help us?"

Was that a flicker of hurt on Anemone's face? "We are still seeing if you're worth helping."

"When you decide we're worth helping, then you get a vote."

Anemone lowered her head, saddened but not showing any inclination to change her mind about being more than an uninvolved observer. "Fair enough. I believe I can speak for Caliban and the nameless ones when I say we'll refrain from insisting on a vote. Besides, we should not participate in this next part, anyway. The inhabitants of that house might be friendly enough to provide you with information, but the barn might present dangers best avoided by my kind."

"Such as what?" Gustav asked.

"The presence of many shadows carries a certain scent, which might . . . awaken sleeping dangers. I offer this advice: Go only to the house, keep the noise to a minimum, and you need never know."

The three nameless shadows didn't offer even that much, but allowed their silence to speak for them. Together, the five shadows who had made their decision to hold off making a decision all stepped back, blurring into a gray mass that seemed to hover in place like a miniature rain cloud that couldn't muster up enough ambition to drop water on something.

"Good to have you along," Fernie muttered. "You're all turning out to be *such* a great help."

But just as she'd written off the idea of any shadow assistance, Olaf advanced, brandishing his sword and jabbing at his chest with his free thumb. "The lady does not speak for me, children. I'll face the danger, if you see fit."

"And I suppose I'll have to, as well," Cousin Cyrus said with a grimace, "just to keep an eye on *this* moron."

He had pointed to Olaf, who bristled with indignation. "That's an insult, sir."

"Good," said Cousin Cyrus. "Then I still know how to make one."

Gustav clapped a palm against his forehead. "Enough! And you, girls? What do you think?"

The What girls glanced at each other to indulge in one of the silent conversations that sisters can have when they're lucky enough to be friends as well as siblings. Neither one needed words to point out to the other that their safety-expert father would not have been happy about their knocking on a strange door in a place they didn't know. Nor did they need words to point out that it was the only door in sight and that they weren't exactly drowning in a sea of other choices. On one hand, how could they take such a foolhardy risk with so much at stake? But on the other hand, how could they not?

Then Pearlie said, "I have a suggestion."

CHAPTER SEVEN
A HOUSE OF BITS AND PIECES

The ridiculously long list of community guidelines that dictated the proper look and colors of houses on Sunnyside Terrace would have curled up in a ball and shriveled had it ever been exposed to the structure Fernie and Pearlie now approached.

The house was big enough to qualify as a mansion by some standards, but was dilapidated and ugly for reasons that went beyond its dull color. It looked like it had been built out of bits and scraps, scavenged from one pile of junk or another, and it seemed like a strong sneeze would have made the boards scatter like dandelion seeds. The house as a whole leaned so far to the left that it seemed to remain standing only out of stubborn habit. If so, it was a habit that it was also giving serious thought to breaking sometime soon.

The house was three stories tall and wide enough in front to accommodate more than forty windows, though they were really just holes where the bits and scraps failed to meet and the only one that emitted any light was the one with the glass lantern on the sill. The barn, separated from the house by the width of one narrow alley, looked more ominous in that more care had been given to its construction and to securing the handles of its great front doors with heavy iron chains. It had a curved roof and was topped with a bell tower, which like the house leaned to one side and seemed about to collapse the first time anybody in the neighborhood stomped a foot. Maybe that was why Anemone had warned the girls to stay away from it. Fernie was still prone to stamping her feet on occasion.

The What sisters approached the front alone, holding hands for reassurance. If there's anything they could have said to each other to make the experience less frightening, anything about not being afraid or being in this together or not worrying as long as they were side by side, it either struck them as too inadequate to say or went without saying, because they covered the entire distance without saying a single word. Every once in a while, one sister faltered and the other sister gave her hand a squeeze, but they each needed that service the same number of times, so it wasn't like either one proved herself any braver than the other.

Then they reached the front door of the house—an imposing wooden slab bearing an iron ring that came equipped with the useful instruction KNOCK. Unfortunately, the ring was set too high in the door for either girl to reach it, an annoying design flaw that obliged Fernie to climb up on her big sister's shoulders, stand on tiptoe, and still find herself unable to reach it. She used her sister's shoulders as a springboard and jumped straight up, knocking Pearlie down in the process. She did manage to seize the bottom of the ring with both hands, but that just left Pearlie on the ground and Fernie dangling from an iron door-knocker she didn't have the leverage to use for its intended purpose.

Lying flat on her back, Pearlie pointed out, "Ow."

"Sorry about that," said Fernie. "A little help, here?"

Pearlie stood, grabbed Fernie by the ankles, and pulled her sister's legs away from the door, finally holding them high above her head so that both Fernie and the iron ring she grasped hung from the wood at the same horizontal angle. Then she let go.

Both Fernie and the door-knocker swung forward, striking the door with a thud that was half iron knocker and half dangling little girl.

Hanging limply against the door, Fernie could only repeat her sister's earlier observation. "Ow."

Fortunately, the girls didn't have to go through that more than once, because the door swung inward with Fernie still hanging from the knocker.

The resident of the house stood revealed, staring down at them. He was a large gap-toothed man the approximate height and shape of a candy vending machine, with massive shoulders, large arms, and a mop of unruly that dangled to his shoulders and mingled with the equally elaborate curls of the beard encircling his chin and jaw. He was as pale as one would expect a man living in the Dark Country to be, but made up for the lack of heavy pigment with the flushed complexion of one who'd just been carrying heavy objects.

His clothes were frayed and worn through in places. It was impossible to see what color they might have been once upon a time, though it looked like horizontal stripes and a convict number might have been involved.

By this time, both Fernie and Pearlie had been without their shadows for so long that it was odd to see a man who was still accompanied by one, even if that shadow didn't drag along the ground as it would have back on Earth, but instead walked upright behind him, its movements staying close to, but not quite matching, his.

"'Allo," the man said, his voice gruff but his manner warm. "This is a nice surprise. Two young shadowless girls, new to the Dark Country."

Fernie released the ring and landed on her feet, backing up a step in case she needed to turn and run in a hurry. "How do you know we're new to the Dark Country?"

"That's downright easy for one who's played host to so many wandering travelers over the years. I can tell that neither one of you has seen any sun in a while, but you both still have the ghost of freckles, fanned out across those cute button noses. Freckles don't last very long in these parts, I fear . . . and, unless they keep their wits about them, neither do little girls." He frowned. "I'm almost surprised to not see a boy and girl instead, given how I hear so many of the evil one's minions are looking for a pair of that description . . . but that doesn't mean I won't provide you with hospitality. Come in, if you'd like."

Neither Fernie nor Pearlie made a move.

The big man didn't take offense. "Come, now. I know nobody glued your little shoes to the ground. This country's known for its odd dangers, but that's not one of them."

It fell to Pearlie to voice the question that had caused the girls to hesitate. "How do we know you're, um . . ."

There seemed no polite word that could be plugged into the empty space at the end of the sentence. But the man provided it. "You were about to say 'harmless'? Well, I'll assure you that it's exactly what I am. I know I'm a stranger and you can't take my word for it, but if you prefer, we can leave the door wide open and you can stay between it and me for as long as it takes you to make up your minds that I'm not about to bake you into any pies."

The man released the door handle and backed away, disappearing into the dim confines of the house. The two What sisters glanced at each other and had another of their silent conversations, admitting to themselves that following him any deeper into his home was a risk, but also conceding that a sensible retreat would amount to traveling this far to learn nothing.

One winding hallway of scraps later they found the man perched on a tiny and wobbly homemade stool in what appeared to be the house's largest room, a place built out of mismatched scraps that was so creepy it cried out for cobwebs, but was somehow even creepier because it didn't have any. His shadow companion sat on a shadow stool beside him with crossed arms. The window with the lantern (not fire, but a little captured ball of sunlight, burning forever in a glass globe) dominated one wall. There were two other lopsided stools, a couple of tarnished rapiers serving as wall decorations, and a shelf bearing three battered hardcover books.

At a loss for anything else to say, Fernie uttered the most untrue words imaginable. "Nice place you have here."

"No, it's not, little miss. It's the best I could do with the bits and pieces that I've been able to scrounge when all the best has to go to maintaining the barn, but it's not a nice place. It's never been a nice place. I do appreciate your saying so, though. How do you like the Dark Country so far?"

"I'm not fond of it," said Fernie.

"Neither am I," Pearlie said, shuddering.

"Or me," the big man said with a sigh. "But alas, here we are."

There was a moment of uncomfortable silence as the girls cast about for another conversation starter.

He saw them glancing at his books. "Ah, those. Every once in a while somebody up in the real world throws an old book into the Pit. That's all I've been able to accumulate since I landed. My collected Shakespeare, my collected Twain, and, unfortunately, given that there's no human food to be had in this dreary place and we'd all starve to death if we didn't have our shadows to eat for us, *The Joy of French Cooking*. I'm afraid I read that one most of all, just to remind myself what a good meal back in the world of light was like. I keep hoping somebody will pass by with something else to read, but alas, it's been years."

"How many years?" Pearlie asked, in a tone that suggested she didn't look forward to knowing.

"The last human event mentioned to me by any of my occasional human visitors was something called the Summer of Love. By then I'd been living in this place almost thirty years, and I'd appreciate it very much if neither one of you fine young ladies tortured me by telling me how many years it's been since then. You'll learn soon enough that time down here doesn't pass the way it does on Earth. It slows down and speeds up, without even the courtesy to separate itself into days and nights so you at least have sensible terms you can use in a conversation. Here, I'm afraid, there are only four terms we use to measure time: *right away*, *soon*, *eventually*, or *never*. Come on, you two. Sit down already. I've long since forgotten how to bite."

Had the man not told them he had been living in the Dark Country for so long, Fernie suspected she would have guessed it from how much sadness filled his every word. She decided that he was more pathetic than dangerous, and that it would be a polite thing to show him a little trust, even if she wasn't quite sure he'd earned it yet.

Fernie lowered herself onto one of the two free stools. It wobbled at once, the way a small dog does when some tiny child tries to ride it. After a moment, she figured out that if she shifted position and leaned to the left, the stool became as stable as it was ever likely to be. "My name's—"

"No names," the big man warned. "That way, if anybody comes looking for you later, I can truthfully say I don't know whether I've seen you or not. It doesn't matter so much what you call me, because it's been so long for me that I've forgotten the name I brought here. I think it started with an *R*." He turned toward his shadow. "Am I right? Did it start with an *R*?"

"It was definitely an *R*," the shadow confirmed, "but I don't remember any more than that."

"Well, let's try some," the big man said. "Ralph? Ruddigore? Ridiculous? Roddenberry?"

The big man's shadow shook his head. "I don't think so."

"Rupert? Revision? Real Estate?"

"No."

"Could it be Roger? Try it."

The shadow pronounced the name with excessive care. "Raaaahhhh-jurrrr."

The big man considered that, then shook his head sadly. "No, I'm afraid that's not it. We might as well use it for the time being, though. I like the sound."

Pearlie, who remained standing, showed signs of losing her patience. "What is this place?"

"This?" He regarded the room around him as if seeing it for the first time. "Ah, well. This is a place I put together from all the bits and pieces I've been able to find so that people would stop by and I would have someone to talk to every once in a while. Welcome to Shadow's Inn."

"You mean . . . it's a hotel?"

"I prefer the term *inn*," said the big man whose name wasn't Roger, "because *hotel* isn't very accurate. Nobody here needs a bed to sleep, so there aren't any guest rooms. What I offer instead is a way station of sorts, for weary travelers both shadow and flesh who wish to pause for congenial company and a friendly voice."

"How often does that happen?"

"You know the name of this place? Not my inn, but the land around it?"

"The Rarely?"

"Well. There you go."

A glum silence followed this pronouncement.

Trying to be helpful, Fernie asked, "Maybe the problem's that you built an inn someplace where guests rarely show up. Wouldn't it be better to have one where folks pass by all the time?"

"If you're doomed to spend your life in the Dark Country," Not-Roger said, "then you'll learn it's best to avoid Dark Country business. I'm better off being lonely and out of trouble than in the center of everything and always fighting for what little life it's possible for me to live. For instance, you two: You may have heard me mention the evil one?"

Fernie said, "Yes. We think we know who you're talking about. We saw the statue. Lord Obsidian, right?"

"That's him. He's a terrible, terrible person, even for the Dark Country, and by far the worst kind of terrible person you ever find here—a shadow who used to be a human being. He's been fighting a brutal war to take over this place and has let it be known that he won't be satisfied until he's also turned the world of light and all the other realms he can reach into places that fit his awful standards. But there's nothing in the Rarely he wants, and so his servants don't pass by here unless they're chasing runaway shadows or whatnot." He sighed again. "Eventually they'll come for me, and I'll have to shut this place down and flee. It's a depressing subject for conversation. Maybe we should talk about something else."

"Why don't we pretend we've covered all the stuff we don't need to talk about and have gotten back to what we can do about Lord Obsidian?"

Not Roger grimaced. "We can't do anything about him. He's too powerful for any of us."

"Let's start with that, then. We already know that he was human when he first landed in the Dark Country. He was just a man named Howard Philip October. How did he go from that to becoming a terrible world-conquering shadow too powerful for anybody to stop?"

Not-Roger rose from his stool, prompting his shadow to rise from his stool so the two could storm over to the other side of the room together. Not-Roger leaned one massive arm on the wall over the window and used that as a resting place for his forehead as he glared at the gray view beyond the light of his little captured sun. His shadow remained behind him.

Neither man nor shadow seemed to notice what Fernie saw: Gustav Gloom just outside ducking out of sight to avoid being spotted.

At Pearlie's suggestion, Gustav had approached the house before the What girls did and taken up his hiding place outside the only window with light so he could stand watch and offer assistance if the man inside proved dangerous. Also not visible in the window at the moment, but no doubt nearby and also listening, were Olaf and Cousin Cyrus.

Apparently unaware just how many eyes were observing him, Not-Roger faced a view he must have known by heart by now and heaved a sigh strong enough to make his whiskers shake. "The truth is, girls, I wasn't a good man back up on Earth. I was a liar and a bully and a thief. Nobody I met was ever better off for knowing me. I've had a long time to think about it, and I confess, I deserved to be thrown in the Pit. I *deserve* to be imprisoned here forever. I wouldn't leave now even if I could.

"But not everybody who's brought here deserves to be here. There's one man in particular, a man who's famous for coming as close to stopping Howard Philip October and the monster he became as anybody ever has. If you want to know how October became Obsidian, his is the story you need to know."

He took another deep breath, long enough for Fernie and—apparently, from the sudden widening of her eyes—Pearlie to realize who he must have been talking about.

Not-Roger said, "His name was Hans Gloom . . ."

CHAPTER EIGHT
THE ORIGIN OF LORD OBSIDIAN

Not-Roger reclaimed his stool, prompting his shadow to do likewise. He sat there absently stroking his beard while he gathered up the bits and pieces of the tale his guests had demanded.

"See, girls, from what I've learned, the world of light has ten Pits to the shadow country. I know one's in Liechtenstein and another's in Orlando, and I hear tell that a third's in a crater somewhere in a place called Tunguska. (That's a bad one.)

"I don't know which one you girls fell through, but I suppose it doesn't matter. You're here to stay, wherever you started off from, because only shadows can travel back and forth unassisted.

"The point is that people from the world of light are always falling through one Pit or another, and most either don't survive very long or don't do much more than wander around losing their minds.

"It was different with those two. Everybody in the Dark Country knew those two were special even before they landed here."

"We knew," Not-Roger's shadow said, "because we could hear them screaming."

Not-Roger nodded. "It's true. No matter where someone was in the Dark Country, in the highest mountaintop or the deepest valley, in the most crowded shadow city or out here in the Rarely, he could hear Hans Gloom and Howard Philip October battling each other as they fell. We all heard every punch, every kick, every groan of pain, and every foul oath they cried as each tried to put an end to the other. We heard Hans Gloom call October a murderer and October call Hans Gloom a naive fool. They never tired and never stopped. It was as if the fight itself was all they had left.

"I don't think there's ever been a pair, in any world, who hated each other that much or who fought each other with that much abandon. Neither one ever stopped to rest, though it took them an uncounted amount of time to fall, and it would have been much easier, in that amount of time, for one to sacrifice his claim on the other."

Not-Roger's shadow shook his head. "It was just two men and their shadows fighting. But you couldn't hear the sounds and not know that the war between them was capable of spreading to entire worlds."

"No," Not-Roger said. "You couldn't." He was silent for a moment, remembering; but then he took a deep breath and continued. "Now, shadows can use one Pit or another to travel back and forth from the world of light faster than it takes a body of flesh and blood to fall, and so a number of them hastened to do just that. They went, gathered information from the shadows of the house where the two men had started their plunge, and reported back what they had learned."

The next minute or so Not-Roger devoted to the parts of the story that he couldn't be aware the girls already knew, beginning with Lemuel Gloom's invention of the Cryptic Carousel many years ago, and continuing past Penny Gloom's murder, to the point where Hans Gloom and Howard Philip October toppled into the Pit together.

Then he moved on to the parts of the story that the girls hadn't heard before.

"You must understand, this wasn't the first time two enemies had ever shared such a fate. It wasn't even the first time two had ever fallen into the Dark Country together. But these two were special. Hans Gloom had been raised in a shadow house and had been saturated with its magic all his life. October had spent long greedy years studying how to exploit the same magic for his own power and was almost as suffused with the same strange forces.

"When they fell, their hands locked around each other's throats, and their shadows also ripped and tore at each other as few enemies had ever fought before. The darkness that already ruled October's soul and the rage that had temporarily taken control of Gloom's made what passed between them a far greater thing than it ever had to be, a greater thing than it ever should have been. Some of the shadows who flew close to watch a part of their fall returned blinded from the fury they had seen.

"The shadows and captive humans of the Dark Country, learning the story of these two enemies, began to fall into several camps. Those who were capable of love, who had known love or who had ever wanted love, felt for Hans Gloom. Those who were ruled by greed, by ambition, by the lust for power, or by hatred of everything that lived felt for Howard Philip October. Others just waited to see what would happen when the pair finally landed, at which point—everybody assumed—one of these two men would triumph over the other and it would no longer be something anyone needed to worry about."

Not-Roger shook his head.

"Some went to watch the landing for themselves. There must have been hundreds of them. My shadow was one; I'd sent him to go take a look. I'll let him take over from there."

Not-Roger's shadow took over. "Gloom and October touched ground on the Golden Desert, a wasteland at the heart of the Dark Country that contains all the riches Man was never meant to find. It's a place where rubies and diamonds the size of houses sit undisturbed, half-buried by sand made out of gold dust. But neither man noticed these treasures, and neither would have cared if they had. Instead, they broke away from each other and rolled in the dirt.

"The men and their shadows scrambled to their feet, facing each other once again.

"They stood apart, eyes burning, enjoying the

first break in the battle as they girded themselves for another round.

"The first to falter was Howard Philip October. The hatred drained from his face, replaced for the moment by total puzzlement. He said, 'It's a shame, Hans. I've never understood you. You lived in a house that offered access to treasures beyond counting and forces that could have granted you power most men will never know . . . and you were ready to squander it, let it all go to waste, just to live the life of an ordinary man. Why?'

"Hans Gloom wiped the sweat from his forehead with the back of his hand. 'Maybe it's because it's all I ever wanted.'

"'You can't win,' October warned him. 'I've been studying how shadow-magic works. I've started to learn how to control it in a way you never can.'

"Hans Gloom's only response to that was a little nod. 'But I have more power than you'll ever know,' he replied.

"Howard Philip October made the mistake of flashing an incredulous look and asking him how.

"Hans Gloom said, 'I have the memory of a wife who honored me by loving me as much as I loved her, and who until the day she died offered you just as great an honor by being your friend. I had a beautiful son who never got the chance to be born and who I never got to meet, who I'll love to the day I die even though I can only love the idea of him. I have the knowledge that you took those people, who were more precious to me than any amount of power, and threw them both away like they were garbage. Do you really imagine that there's any force, in this world or any other, that's strong enough to prevent me from avenging either one of them, even if it's with my very last breath?' "

As Not-Roger's shadow let the words ring, Fernie's vision blurred with tears, and she thought of poor Gustav listening to this story from his hiding place. It was breaking her own heart. What was it doing to him, the halfsie boy who had never before experienced the chance to hear his father profess his love for him?

Pearlie pointed out what Fernie had not. "But wasn't Hans wrong about his son? Gustav Gloom *did* get to be born. He did get to be more than an idea. He did get to be a person."

Not-Roger nodded. "True, miss . . . as all who know this terrible history recognize. But at the particular time this story took place, Hans Gloom had no way of knowing it. He still believed that his unborn son had perished at the same time as his poor wife. As far as he was concerned, then and for a long time afterward, Howard Philip October had taken his entire family from him, not just half of it."

"I hope he eventually found out otherwise," Pearlie said.

"That I don't know," Not-Roger said, while dabbing at his shiny eyes with a thumb. "But I hope so, too."

His shadow resumed the tale. "In any event, what happened next, and what I had the privilege to witness, became a legend among my kind.

"Hans Gloom and his shadow started to walk.

"They took a step and then a step after that and then a third step after that one, each one bringing them closer to Howard Philip October.

"The look in Gloom's eyes was the worst and most frightening thing I have ever seen.

"All the shadows watching the moment thought that Howard Philip October and his shadow would advance to meet Gloom in the middle and that the fight between them would start all over again.

"But that's not what happened.

"Instead, October and his shadow turned their backs and started to run.

"They ran and stumbled and fell flat on their faces and crawled and got up and started to stagger away again.

"Behind them, Hans Gloom and his shadow never sped up and never hurried and never broke into a run to close the distance, but also never stopped; they just kept walking, putting one foot ahead of the other for as long as Howard Philip October and his shadow fled.

"I didn't stick around much longer after that. But Hans Gloom and his shadow were pitiless. They never stopped to rest. They never sped up to end it. They just walked at the same merciless, unhurried pace . . . and for as long as they walked, there was nothing Howard Philip October and his shadow could do to escape.

"I don't think Gloom intended to kill October anymore. Instead, he dedicated himself to doing something that might be considered even worse—denying his enemy even a moment of rest, or peace, for as long as his own strength permitted him.

"There were times when October was able

to put some distance between them and Gloom was just a small dot he had left far behind; and there were times when October had to stop to rest and watch while Gloom approached almost close enough to reach out and touch him. There were times October was just out of Gloom's reach for what would have been days on end back in the world of light, and they were able to have extended conversations. From what I hear from those who stuck around long enough to see what was going to happen, October desperately offered Gloom one deal or another to go away, and Gloom replied with loving stories of his life with the woman named Penny.

"They trekked through deserts, through shadow cities, over mountains, past even the lair of monsters who would have attacked and eaten anybody else, but who must have sensed that this pair and their shadows were better off left alone. If this had happened in the world of light, somebody would have dropped from hunger or thirst or exhaustion . . . but both these men had shadows who departed from time to time to scavenge food or rest before returning. For the men, there was nothing but the chase to occupy them. So this went on for the equivalent of years . . . and for a long, long time in the Dark Country, the one spoken of with fear was not Howard Philip October, but the furious husband named Hans Gloom, who would never give up, not for a moment."

Not-Roger sighed. "If only he'd walked a little faster! If only he'd ended that evil man while it was still possible!"

"But he did not," Not-Roger's shadow replied, "and those who paid attention to the endless chase started to remark on something that grew ever more disturbing as time went on."

"October seemed to be losing weight," Not-Roger continued.

"It was not the kind of weight a man can lose by walking long distances. It was more than that. October had not been a fat man to start, but what little meat there was to him seemed to be wasting away with every step he took. His skin started hanging loosely on his frame. Before long it was like an overlarge borrowed suit, with wrinkles and folds and flaps and more hanging loose than seemed even close to ever having fit. Have you girls ever seen a man who's forgotten his belt and had to use his hand to keep his pants from falling down? October grew to be like that . . . except that it was the skin of his legs that he had to hold on to, to keep it from slipping off his bones.

"Despite this, October walked like a man who was getting stronger, not weaker . . . and when his eyes finally turned jet-black, those who watched knew that something unnatural had happened inside him. He became so terrible that even his shadow fled, to some part of the Dark Country not known—and no one, flesh or shadow, has seen him in all the years since.

"When the transformation was complete, October turned around, faced Hans Gloom from a mere ten paces away, and let his skin fall to the ground, like a bathrobe he had decided to discard. He simply stepped out of his old self, leaving it on the ground behind him, and stood revealed as the creature he had become, the shadow who would soon come to be known and feared as Lord Obsidian.

"The sight was terrible enough for that first look to make Hans Gloom and his shadow stop their endless march for the first time in more miles than can possibly be counted and fall to their knees in horror.

"Lord Obsidian said, 'You have waited too long, Hans. You have lost your chance at revenge. Instead, I have become what I always sought to become . . . and I shall do what I have always vowed to do. I will raise an army. I will conquer this place. I will storm the world of light, as well, and make it my own. And if you wonder why I do not kill you now, it is because I want nothing more than for you to see it and know that you could have prevented it.'

"He bent over, scooped up the skin he had shed as if he still had use for it, and rose laughing into the gray sky . . . while the good man he had long fled was left on the ground, weeping."

The story didn't sound like it was over, but Not-Roger's shadow seemed to have told as much of it as his heart would bear right now. His head dipped until his bearded chin rested on his barrel chest, and he sat there, silently brooding over his nested fingers, as if remembering events that had once happened to him.

Fernie was just as silent, because she realized she knew what had happened to the skin the man October had shed. Filled with captured shadows, and still using the name Howard Philip October, that skin had become the terrible creature she and Gustav came to know as the shadow eater and had only a few weeks ago invaded the Gloom house on a brutal search for an artifact Lord Obsidian wanted.

The oppressive silence began to feel like a weight resting on all their heads, until Pearlie said, "I don't get it. That kind of thing doesn't just happen. People don't just step out of their skins and become someone else."

"This is the Dark Country," Not-Roger grumbled. "Shadow-magic happens here."

"But why didn't it happen to Hans Gloom? He walked the exact same distance!"

"Ah, well. Some of Lord Obsidian's followers say that it's because Howard Philip October was the one born to greatness."

"But that's not what you think," Pearlie said.

"No, girl, I don't. I think Howard Philip October was just a selfish, evil man, and that Lord Obsidian is just the same man in shadow form. Here's my explanation: The more he was denied what he wanted, the more that greed and hate festered inside him, the more it ate him up and replaced everything he was with darkness. When there was no longer enough of him to keep his skin on, only the shadow he wanted to be, Lord Obsidian, was left. Hans Gloom was also driven by hate, but it was the kind of hate caused by knowing that the man before him had robbed him of everybody he loved . . . and there was enough of that love left, reminding him of why he fought so hard, to keep that same transformation from happening to him. A rotten person could choose to believe that Hans's love for his family made him weak. But it's not something I'm willing to say."

It wasn't anything Fernie was willing to say, either. As far as she was concerned, the story showed only that Hans Gloom had kept a part of himself even in the Dark Country that Howard Philip October had lost long before he ever got there. But the thought reminded her of Gustav, who must have heard all this from his hiding place right outside the window, and again, her heart broke a little at the very idea.

She didn't look forward to the rest of the story, which would no doubt explain how Lord Obsidian had raised his army and what happened to Hans Gloom in the meantime. She didn't think she could take it.

But as it happened, she wasn't going to get a chance to hear that part of the story right away, because somebody outside started screaming.

CHAPTER NINE
LUNGS ARE NOT INVOLVED

There are sounds that come naturally when two men throw everything they have into battling each other. They include punches landing on noses, kicks landing in worse places, gasps of pain exchanged just to establish the point system, shouted variations on the worst names anybody could ever possibly call another, and hideous growls added just to underline that all of this was done with significant enthusiasm.

Cousin Cyrus's gravelly voice rose to an irritated whine. "Get off me, you self-mythologizing miscreant!"

The other voice belonged to Olaf, who cried, "Not while a breath of air remains in my lungs, you foul degenerate!"

"That's what I mean when I call you an idiot, you idiot! You're a shadow! You don't even have lungs!"

The ensuing thud rattled the ceiling of Shadow's Inn so hard that the walls trembled and sagged ever closer to total collapse.

Not-Roger cried, "The noise!"

Man and shadow were off their stools and well on their way to the door, passing the startled What girls. Both had already left the inn by the time the girls reached the outside. When they did, Fernie was out the door a fraction of a second after Pearlie and knew from her sister's appalled upward gaze where to look for the source of the fighting.

The battle between Olaf and Cousin Cyrus had reached the inn's roof. Olaf had drawn his sword to slash at Cousin Cyrus with a fury that would have carved a flesh-and-blood man into segments. It had the same effect, more or less, on Cousin Cyrus. Each swing cut him in half and left the two parts separated by the width of the slash before they came back together and rejoined just in time to be cut in half again.

Though the wounds didn't seem to cause Cousin Cyrus any pain, he wasn't happy about them, either, and cursed with irritation every time he was halved.

Whenever he could, Cousin Cyrus leaped

past the sword's cutting range to pummel Olaf's face with his shadowy fists. These didn't seem to hurt Olaf all that much, either, but each blow reduced Olaf's already unlovely features to a crater, which each time popped back into place just in time for Cousin Cyrus to crater it again with another punch.

Gustav was nowhere to be seen. He had probably ducked around the corner of the inn to avoid being seen by Not-Roger. And now the fight had grown so violent that bits and pieces of the inn's roof crumbled and tumbled to the ground as debris.

Anemone, the robed Caliban, and the three nameless other shadows of the party were all dots on the horizon, watching from a safe distance with what struck Fernie as bland disinterest. But Not-Roger noted the small mob of shadows now standing around in a place so isolated that even shadows rarely showed their faces here, and he asked Fernie, "Are those friends of yours?"

Fernie saw no good reason to deny it now. "More or less. I wouldn't call any of them *friends*." She thought about it. "Except Olaf, maybe. He seems to have his heart in the right place, at least."

"You stupid girl!" This came from Cousin Cyrus, who lifted his teeth from Olaf's ear long enough to shout a cranky warning. "He doesn't have his heart in the right place! He's a *spy* for Lord Obsidian!"

"I'm no spy!" Olaf cried. "You're the spy!"

Not-Roger sidestepped to avoid a piece of scrap wood dislodged by the battle, which tumbled downward spinning like a boomerang and embedded itself in the dirt at his feet. "Either one of them could be a spy," he noted, not seeming to take the damage to his home at all seriously. "You could be a spy. I could be a spy. Any one of those other shadows could be a spy. This country's at war. In wartime, you can't throw a rock in any random direction without hitting a spy. For all I know, all of you are spies."

"Maybe none of us are spies," Pearlie countered.

"That's also a possibility," said Not-Roger. "The only thing that's never going to happen here is none of us ever being accused of being a spy, because in a war, everybody gets treated like a spy whether they are or not."

Up above, Olaf and Cousin Cyrus had grabbed hold of each other's ears and used them as handles to shake each other's heads, a tactic that made both forget where they were and sent both on an unstoppable biting-and-gouging roll down the inn's sloping roof. They fell together over the side, plummeted together toward the ground, and hit the earth together with an impact that hurt neither but still raised a cloud of dust. Fernie and Pearlie and Not-Roger erupted into coughing fits, but the same dust didn't silence shadows who didn't need to breathe in order to speak. Olaf and Cousin Cyrus continued to accuse each other of being spies even as the clouds around them continued to swirl.

"I would break in," Not-Roger's shadow remarked, "but I don't know which one is telling the truth."

The dust dispersed. Cousin Cyrus lay facedown on the ground, throwing punches at dirt he imagined had Olaf in it. But Olaf had slipped away and scrambled back up to the roof, where he now retrieved his shadow sword, got his bearings, and stood for a moment, posing against the gray sky. He thrust his chin out and began to lope along the roof, headed in the direction of the barn. Something had changed about his posture. He no longer looked like a shadow trying to live up to the memory of a human hero; he looked like one who knew exactly what he was here for and was determined to get on with it.

"Oh no," said Not-Roger.

"He's headed for the barn!" said Not-Roger's shadow.

Fernie remembered Anemone's dire warnings about the barn. "What's in the barn?"

"Never mind what's *in* the barn," Not-Roger snapped. "It's still asleep, at least. Worry more right now about what's *on* the barn!"

The only thing on the barn was the bell tower, which suddenly seemed to loom tall as the most dangerous location in the vicinity.

It was no longer funny that two peculiar and half-crazy shadows bickered over who was and who wasn't a spy. There was no telling what would happen to any of them if Olaf reached the barn and succeeded in ringing that bell.

Fernie started to run, pacing Olaf as well as she could, but falling behind with every step because he was a shadow capable of a shadow's speed and she was a human being who could run only as fast as legs could move.

Olaf reached the gap between the inn and the barn, and with almost no effort at all leaped the distance, alighting on the barn as gently as a snowflake landing on a leaf.

For a fraction of a second he seemed to cast a shadow of his own. It made the leap just behind him, but was oddly smaller than he was and made an audible *thwap* when it hit the same roof.

Fernie's heart leaped when she realized that the smaller shadow was not a shadow at all, but a boy in black who had somehow made it to rooftop level to pursue Olaf as only he could.

Any doubts she might have had about Olaf turning out to be an enemy went away as he whirled in place and thrust his shadow sword at Gustav's belly.

Gustav darted backward to avoid the strike, and for one very terrible heartbeat teetered on the edge of the roof, pinwheeling his arms to resist what might have been a fatal fall. This presented an irresistible target for Olaf, who came after him with another thrust. Gustav, who was not actually off balance at all, neatly sidestepped the sword, spun around Olaf's back, and kicked the attacking shadow in his backside. The kick didn't knock Olaf over the edge, but did make him stumble and leave a huge dent in his rear end, which made him look extraordinarily silly and slowed him down enough for Gustav to kick him again.

Down below, Not-Roger stopped in his tracks, his mouth falling so far open that it almost qualified as a wonder that his jaw didn't pop a rivet and fall off. "My word! That's Gustav Gloom!"

Fernie figured the secret was out. "Uh-huh."

"B-but . . ." With equal amazement, Not-Roger turned to Pearlie. "That means *you* must be Fernie What!"

"Nope," said Pearlie. "I'm just her older and even tougher sister, Pearlie."

Not-Roger's shadow blinked a number of times in rapid succession. "There's a *tougher* sister?"

Up on the barn roof, the dent in Olaf's rear end popped back out. Outraged, he slashed at Gustav again, his shadow sword flashing with a swing of the sort he'd repeatedly used to cut Cousin Cyrus in half. The damage Olaf had done on those occasions had been temporary, because Cousin Cyrus was a shadow who had no blood that could be spilled. There was no telling what would happen to Gustav if a swing just like it struck home. Gustav seemed to know it, too, because he leaped over the slash and let it pass by harmlessly underneath him.

Down below, Not-Roger clutched Fernie by the shoulders. "You can't be here, girl, not any of you! Haven't you heard that Lord Obsidian's put special priority on catching you lot?"

"Yes, we did hear that," Fernie said. "But here we are anyway."

Up above, Olaf screeched with rage as Gustav remained just out of his reach, but got control of his sudden seeming hatred of the halfsie boy and seemed to remember whatever he knew about swordplay. Instead of wild, uncontrolled swings, he concentrated on short, on-target jabs, each of them aimed at Gustav's heart. Gustav could only dodge these by retreating, one step at a time, but each retreat brought Olaf closer to the bell tower that seemed to be his goal. Long before that, Gustav would be trapped with a wall at his back.

Cousin Cyrus, who had risen back to rooftop level while the girls and the shadows were giving all their attention to the fight, wrapped his arms around Olaf's neck and managed to pull him a few steps away from Gustav.

Olaf spun in his grip. The sword slashed,

separating Cousin Cyrus's head from his shoulders. This was no more fatal or permanent than any of the other damage Olaf's sword had done, but it was effective at getting rid of Cousin Cyrus for a while. His headless body fell backward and came apart like a puff of smoke, while his head sailed off behind the inn, loudly complaining about the nonsense he had to suffer through whenever somebody forced him to get involved.

Fernie still didn't fully understand why Cousin Cyrus would fight so hard for the life of a boy he claimed to despise, but she didn't have time to stop and think about it right now.

Instead, she declared, "Nerts to this."

She twisted her way out of Not-Roger's grasp and ran back along the wall to the inn's entrance. A quick stop inside and she emerged carrying the two tarnished rapiers she had seen hanging from the study wall. She held each from the grip under its curved hand guard and looked like a girl ready to engage in swordplay herself, though she had never once held a sword of any kind in her hand and had gotten all of her practice at the sport dueling her sister with yardsticks.

Not-Roger was very put out that two of his

possessions had just been drafted as weaponry. "Hey. Those are mine."

Fernie handed the rapier in her left hand to her sister, who immediately cut the air with a whining slash just to test it out. "Sorry. They're not worth as much to you as my friend is to me. I'll pay you back if I have a chance. What's the fastest way to the barn roof?"

"You can't join the fight," Not-Roger's shadow protested. "The more people on the roof, the noisier it gets!"

"It's noisy now!" Fernie snapped.

"You can't let it get any noisier!"

Fernie didn't see why the noise made any particular difference, but she said, "It's going to be a lot louder than this if that bell rings!"

Not-Roger fell back, his mouth agape at the very prospect.

There was a thud from up above as Gustav leaped from one part of the roof to another in order to evade one of Olaf's attacks.

Fernie met Not-Roger's eyes. "See? It's getting noisier already. *Somebody* has to go up there to help Gustav . . . and we're lighter than you, so our footsteps won't be as loud."

Looking like there were about a million

places in and out of the Dark Country that he would rather be, Not-Roger finally told her, "There's a ladder! I'll show you."

Fernie hated taking her eyes off the battle, but she had to in order to follow Not-Roger down the narrow patch of dirt between the inn and the barn and around the corner to the rear, where the innkeeper proudly pointed out what he had meant by *ladder*.

It turned out to be a collection of ramshackle boards of different sizes and shapes, nailed directly to the barn at varying angles in a manner that she supposed qualified as a ladder in the same way that the wreck of an inn qualified as a house. Fernie couldn't trust any of the boards not to pull free as soon as she rested any of her weight on them, and she knew that being one-handed because of the rapier would make the climb even more clumsy and treacherous than it already was. But it wasn't like she had any other choice. It was the only way to get to Gustav.

She was about to reach for the ladder when Pearlie gently pushed her aside.

"Just this once," Pearlie said, "let me be the big sister and go first."

There was no particular reason why Fernie

should have been surprised by this. But right now, Pearlie's brave offer threw her off so much that she didn't argue. She just stepped back and let Pearlie climb first.

Pearlie raced up the ladder one-handed and clambered up onto the barn roof in less time than would have taken some people to cross the street. Fernie was just a few rungs behind her and saw one of the highest rungs bend under Pearlie's sneaker, but there was no time to be careful, not with her sister and best friend under attack by a crazy shadow swordsman, so she just pushed on.

She made the mistake of grabbing the loose rung with her one free hand.

It pulled free, and she started to fall . . .

CHAPTER TEN
NEVER GET PEARLIE WHAT MAD

Fernie felt the terrible bone-shattering fall about to happen and knew not just that she was about to be terribly hurt, but that her absence in the battle would mean a fate worse than death for everybody whose future absolutely depended on her not doing anything stupid like falling off a barn.

But then a sour muttering wind blew against her back, pushing her upright and giving her a chance to grab hold of the next board higher up.

"This is why I don't like people," muttered Cousin Cyrus's head as it released her and sailed past her, trailing a puffy black tail that made him look like the negative image of a comet. "They're just so much trouble all the time."

Fernie refrained from pointing out that her introduction to the world of shadows hadn't made her life all that easy. Instead she scrambled up and over the edge of the barn roof and saw the rapier she'd given Pearlie now firmly clutched in the hand of Gustav Gloom.

Pearlie, who must have tossed him the weapon as soon as she reached the top, now hugged the roof to stay out of his way while he did what needed to be done.

As it happened, swordplay seemed to be yet another skill Gustav had managed to pick up in his long years of living in a house with no other people and only indifferent shadows for company. Even as Fernie spotted him, he parried a thrust aimed at his heart and used his own weapon to drive the shadow swordsman back, away from the bell tower and toward the gap between the two buildings.

As much as she ached to help Gustav herself, Fernie managed to resist entering the fray. She just cheered, "Get 'im, Gustav!"

Down below, Not-Roger's shadow cried, "Your enthusiasm will be the death of you, girl! *Keep the noise down!*"

Elsewhere on the roof, Cousin Cyrus's head reunited with his body. He immediately collapsed into a clumsy snit because he'd been in such a terrible hurry to put himself together that he'd foolishly attached his head backward. He grabbed himself by the ears and tried to wrench it back into its proper attitude, but it seemed to be jammed in its current location. He *aaarrrghed* as he tugged louder.

Backed up against the gap, the suddenly villainous Olaf lowered his sword in what amounted to a respectful salute. "You're good, boy. You're very good. But you may have noticed I'm smiling. Don't you want to know why?"

Gustav touched the tip of his rapier to Olaf's neck. "Are you about to tell me you're not really left-handed?"

Confusion flickered over Olaf's features. After a moment, he recovered and said, "No! It's because I'm a shadow and nothing you do with your sword can really hurt me! All you've managed to do is make this fight interesting for a few minutes. I can take a break from destroying you all just long enough to amuse myself by telling you exactly why you'll never be anything but a stupid and gullible boy."

Gustav blinked. "Oh good. I love stories."

"Nothing I told you about my past was true! I was plotting to betray you all along, and you never even had a clue!"

Gustav did something that Fernie had only seen him do a few times: He smiled. It was as always an odd smile, in that it indicated genuine amusement without ever affecting his sad and lonely eyes. "Don't be silly. I knew it from the very first moment I saw you."

Olaf snarled like a cat confronted by an intruder in his territory. "You lie. You want me to think you can't be fooled!"

"Oh, I can be fooled," Gustav said without much concern. "I've been fooled a number of times. I just can't be fooled by anybody who does such a terrible job of fooling me."

Olaf lunged. "You lie!"

Gustav parried the strike without any difficulty at all and left Olaf teetering on the edge again. "Think about it. I always knew that when I asked those refugees for help, I was almost certainly going to get at least one shadow out of that crowd less interested in helping us than in making friends with the side that seems to be winning. That wasn't hard to figure out. In any fight, there's always somebody only interested in helping himself. All I had to do was figure out who it was and keep an eye on that one."

"You still haven't said why you expect me

to believe you suspected me and not any of the others."

"I don't care what you believe," Gustav said, "but I might as well explain it to you, because it's really very simple. You see, any halfway decent *spy* does whatever he can to make sure that the people he's spying on trust him. That's the very definition of a spy's *job*."

"So?"

"So Anemone, Caliban, and the three without names didn't do that at all. They didn't care whether I trusted them or not. They didn't claim to be on our side or agree to take our orders. Instead, they all said that they expected us to get killed or captured before long, and that they might change their minds and help us if we didn't. By offering me absolutely no reason to trust them, they gave me every *possible* reason to trust them.

"You, on the other hand? You offered us your help, made sure we considered you the harmless shadow of some ancient knight who was only dangerous because he smelled bad, and did everything you possibly could to make friends. You *cared* whether we trusted you. So I knew it was only a matter of time before you gave us a reason to stop trusting you. If a betrayal was coming, it was always coming from you."

Olaf's face flickered. It wasn't the flicker of somebody making an important decision, but the flicker of a mask faltering, a true face deciding whether to come out. For a second his features seemed to melt at the edges. "Why not Cousin Cyrus? He's not exactly shy about how much he despises you."

Elsewhere on the roof, Cousin Cyrus was busy trying to twist his head in the right direction, but it was firmly stuck in place, like the cap on a brand-new bottle of ketchup. He grumbled, "At least somebody's paying attention. I was worried I wasn't being clear enough."

Gustav's lips twitched. "I don't like Cousin Cyrus any more than he likes me. Nobody who *knows* him likes him. But I understand him. I know that if he says he's here paying off a debt to my great-aunt Mellifluous, he's paying off a debt to Great-Aunt Mellifluous, because debts are the only thing he's ever taken seriously. Besides, he's not exactly about to betray me to Lord Obsidian, even if he does hate me, because if he ever does that, then he'll have to *keep* working for Lord Obsidian . . . and you only have to listen to him for five minutes to know that it's more work than he's ever been interested in doing. So I trusted him from the very beginning."

Cousin Cyrus was now on his hands and knees, banging his off-kilter head against the roof in the apparent hopes that a good knock would loosen it. "You know, I really could use some help here."

Olaf lowered his sword to his side and turned his poisonous gaze on Fernie and Pearlie. "Well, at least I fooled the girls. I *always* fool the girls. Those ninnies *still* don't know who I am."

Fernie had in fact only deduced who Olaf really was a few seconds ago, but figured it wouldn't hurt to pretend she'd known longer. "Not true. You didn't fool me for long the first time we met, when you pretended to be the shadow of a lonely little girl. You didn't fool me for long the second time we met, when you pretended to be Gustav. He's right about you. You talk big, but you really aren't very good at this."

The corners of Olaf's snarl turned up until they had almost reached his ears, at which point they connected and formed a seam that went all the way around his head. Everything above those lips popped off in a puff of smoke and a new face emerged, this one the visage of a five-year-old girl wearing ringlets and bows. It was the kind of face that should have been angelic and adorable, but failed both measurements because it was impossible to look at it without knowing that it belonged to the kind of child who was just plain rotten.

This couldn't be considered Olaf's true face, because the shadow he really was changed shapes so often that it was impossible to consider any of his many faces more true than any other. But even as he shrunk two feet and grew a puffy, ankle-length dress in place of his previous chain-mail armor, the transformation itself marked him as a shadow criminal Fernie had encountered twice. The last time Fernie had seen him, the leader of the vicious shadow gang known as the Four Terrors had been fleeing into the Pit to avoid being captured alongside his three partners.

She lifted her own rapier in salute. "Hello, Nebuchadnezzar."

Pearlie stared at the sneering little girl with the fiercest expression Fernie had ever seen on her face. "That's Nebuchadnezzar? That's the shadow who got us all into this mess?"

Now strictly speaking, it wasn't quite Nebuchadnezzar's fault that Fernie's father and sister had fallen into the Pit by accident a few minutes after his hasty departure, but he was still responsible for threatening their lives in the first place.

"Yes," Gustav said. "This is Nebuchadnezzar."

Pearlie leaped to her feet in fury. The adventure hadn't been easy on any of them, but unlike Gustav and Fernie, she hadn't started it with a week of mostly quiet journeying aboard the Cryptic Carousel or with the comfort of friends to share the dangers with her. Until being reunited with Gustav and her sister, she'd had little but fear and loss in a dark and unpleasant place, and all of it burned in her eyes now as she faced down the shadow who had done so much to cause it. She gestured at Fernie's rapier. "Gimme that."

Fernie said, "You don't have to. Gustav's already—"

"I'm not *asking*. Give it to me."

Fernie handed the rapier over with no further argument.

Pearlie whipped the blade through the air before her to test its weight and make it sing.

A couple of vicious test swings and she satisfied herself that she was ready. "You think it's *funny* to kidnap good men and little girls? You think it's nice to hand them to guys who *take* people, or threaten to drop them into bottomless pits? You think that's *enjoyable*? Would your life be *boring* otherwise?"

"Yes," said Nebuchadnezzar. "Thanks for asking."

Pearlie took a single angry step, her grip on the rapier's handle turning her knuckles white. "Did you really think you could just go around doing that kind of thing without ever being punished for it?"

Nebuchadnezzar's rotten little girl face split open, revealing yet another face beneath it. This one was a cruel caricature of Pearlie that made her eyes look moronic, her freckles look like disgusting blotches, and her mouth look like a gaping, toothless hole that could only hang open in idiocy. "What do you think you're going to do about it? I'm a shadow, and that's just a rapier! You can use it to keep me at bay for a few minutes, or even slice me up like I sliced up Cyrus, but there's no way you'll ever be able to use it to hurt me!"

Gustav still held his own rapier's point at Nebuchadnezzar's neck. Without turning around, he said, "He has a point, Pearlie. I'm better at this than you are, but you can't mistake what I've done for defeating him. This fight begins again the second he decides he wants it to begin again."

Pearlie's eyes narrowed with an even deeper fury. "Don't make the same mistake he's made, Gustav. I'm not stupid. I've seen what this weapon can and can't do to shadows. But I never planned to use it on *him*."

She drew the rapier back over her shoulder and swung it with all her might.

What she'd decided to do might not have required all her might, given her target, but putting everything she had into it must have made the result just a little bit more satisfying.

Her target wasn't Nebuchadnezzar, who she hadn't even bothered to approach.

It was Cousin Cyrus.

Once again his head popped off, the same way a flesh-and-blood head would have. But this time, instead of sailing over the edge of the roof, it just spun three times to orient itself and then sank down upon his neck, this time facing the proper direction.

Cousin Cyrus tilted his restored head one way and then the other to test it, his neck providing an audible crack even though it didn't contain the bones normally required to make that noise. "Ahhh. That's *much* better."

"I'm glad," said Pearlie, who didn't sound like she was very glad at all. "But I didn't do it because I consider us friends. I did it because now *you owe me one*."

Cousin Cyrus froze in dismay, because he hadn't considered that. "I don't owe you anything, girlie. I've already done more than enough for you."

Pearlie's reply was as cold as anything Fernie had ever heard her say. "That's not the way I figure it. Everything you've ever done for me you did for Great-Aunt Mellifluous. I know you're still paying off that debt and can't just put it down like you want to, but now this small part of it belongs only to *me*. You want to pay me back?" She whipped around and pointed the tip of the rapier at Nebuchadnezzar. "*Make this piece of garbage sorry for a long, long time.*"

Nebuchadnezzar looked startled. "What?"

Cousin Cyrus moaned the same moan Fernie had once heard from an old man whose bag of groceries had just split open and spilled all over the sidewalk, obliging him to bend over and clean up the mess. "That's unfair. I was fighting him already before I lost my head."

"Well, now," Pearlie said, without any sympathy at all, "I've fixed your head, and now you can fight him some more. And this time, you can fight him as if your own life depended on it. Fight him the way you would if you loved us. Fight him the way you would if you hated nothing in the world more than you hated him. Fight him until he's something none of us have to worry about, ever again. Do that, Cousin Cyrus, and *then* the two of us will be even."

"Oh boy," said Gustav.

Cousin Cyrus muttered under his breath, because this really was the worst of all the infernal impositions he'd had to deal with so far. But a debt was a debt, and so he hauled himself to his feet, moaning with every stretch as if it were the worst trouble anybody had ever put him to.

He then became a gray blur.

It was the fastest any of them had ever seen him move, faster than any of them had ever imagined he *could* move.

Gustav dove out of the way just before the

impact, which was a good thing, because the tackle was downright explosive. The edge of the barn roof shattered into a small cloud of tiny splinters, and a second later the nearest wall of the inn did as well, as Cousin Cyrus's tackle sent both shadow bodies smashing into its side. A further wave of dust and debris erupted out of the hole, followed by the kind of sounds that would not have been out of place coming from a building whose owners had decided to shatter all their crockery with sledgehammers.

A distant cry cut through the air. It was Anemone, still standing with her companions at the safe distance she'd insisted upon, reacting with horror at the noise she'd warned Gustav and the Whats to avoid at all cost.

Fernie was impressed. "Remind me to never get you mad," she said to her sister.

Pearlie handed back the rapier. "You're my little sister. You learned that lesson long ago."

Part of the inn's roof collapsed and then exploded, bits and pieces of the junk it was made of erupting upward like a geyser made of scrap. But it wasn't the only building in trouble. The damage done to the barn roof, which was already rattling the bell in its tower, caused tremors that Fernie could feel up and down her legs. She fell to her knees as, below her, something that didn't sound very nice at all protested this disturbance with the kind of snarl that promised very large and very painful bites to anybody responsible.

This was not a sound Fernie ever wanted to be near, particularly on occasions when she was also near a pair of crazy shadows furiously battling over the right to ring mysterious bells. "What was that?"

From far away came Anemone's answering cry: "Children! Get down from there now!"

"Why?" Gustav yelled back. "What's happening?"

Not-Roger provided the despairing answer: "You've woken my gnarfle!"

Even as the barn rattled again from the shock waves of the battle inside the inn, the three visitors from Sunnyside Terrace exchanged worried glances.

Pearlie bit her lip. "I didn't mean to wake up a gnarfle."

Fernie said, "I would have liked to find out exactly what a gnarfle was first."

"Given the way our luck usually runs,"

Gustav said, "I pretty much expected it to come up sooner or later."

Across the alley, Shadow's Inn rattled and swayed from the violent struggles inside. But the barn shook even more as something trapped under its roof screeched and pounded the walls. Terrible things might have been happening to both places, but there was really no contest which threatened bigger problems, because as vicious as the renewed battle between Nebuchadnezzar and Cousin Cyrus had become, whatever stirred in the barn was clearly far more powerful and far more angry. One of its blows against the barn walls was so strong that the roof seemed to jump off the rest of the structure and then settle back slightly out of place, like a wig worn at the wrong angle. Gustav managed to hold on, but Fernie and Pearlie were both thrown off their feet and sent tumbling down the curve of the roof toward the edge.

This was the second time Fernie found herself threatened by a probable fall off this particular building in the last few minutes. All in all, she didn't see anything in this second exposure to the experience that improved the poor opinion she'd had of it the first time.

She shrieked and scrambled for a handhold, but holding on was next to impossible given how badly the entire structure was shaking, and so she continued to roll until her legs slipped over the edge and she found herself clawing at a roof that seemed to be disintegrating in her hands.

Just before she fell, she saw Gustav dive across the roof and catch Pearlie, who was closer, by the wrist. *That's good,* she thought. *But I need to be rescued, too.*

But even Gustav couldn't be in two places at the same time, and so she fell over the side. Tumbling into open space, she found herself absolutely certain that this wasn't going to end well at all.

CHAPTER ELEVEN
THE CARE AND FEEDING OF YOUR PET GNARFLE

Just as Fernie prepared herself for a bone-rattling collision with the ground, two massive arms appeared out of nowhere and caught her, plucking her from her plunge with an ease that made Fernie wonder just how practiced Not-Roger was in catching people who fell off rooftops in his vicinity.

Instead of saying something reassuring like "Don't worry, I've got you" or "It's all right, you're safe now" or any other sequence of words that might give comfort to somebody who had just fallen off a roof, Not-Roger winced and said, "Ow. My poor back's going to be complaining about that one."

Fernie didn't say what's normally expected of a person in this situation, either. She could have said "Thank you" or "My hero" or "You saved my life" or even "I'm sorry about your back."

Instead, she rolled out of Not-Roger's arms, landed in a crouch, and rose, crying, "What are you doing with a *gnarfle*, whatever that is, in your *barn*?"

Not-Roger averted his eyes. "I'm lonely."

"For a gnarfle? Again, *whatever that is*?"

He shrugged. "It's not like I get all that many opportunities to pop off to the neighborhood pet shop for a goldfish."

"There aren't any neighborhood pet shops in the Dark Country," his shadow confirmed.

The unseen creature inside the barn emitted another ear-piercing bellow and slammed the walls of its prison yet again. The impact was great enough to make the ground shake. Fernie fell to her knees. Not-Roger braced himself, took a step to his immediate right, and plucked the plummeting figures of Gustav Gloom and Pearlie What from the air, again with an expressive wince over whatever strain this operation put on his lower back.

Either Gustav or Fernie or Pearlie would have chosen this moment to ask him what a gnarfle was, but that had to wait, as the viciously entwined figures of Nebuchadnezzar and Cousin Cyrus shot past all of them in a blur.

Nebuchadnezzar had taken the form of a giant python, and multiple coils of his long sinuous body were wrapped tight around Cousin Cyrus. Cousin Cyrus had his right arm elbow-deep in Nebuchadnezzar's mouth, as if trying to grab his enemy by some interior place and tug him inside out. They skipped across the ground like a flat stone tossed across the surface of a placid lake, raising a little cloud of dust with each impact as they receded into the far distance.

A few months earlier, this would have been the most remarkable thing that either What girl had ever seen. It would have been the subject of frenzied discussion for weeks, if not months, afterward. They might have continued to discuss this really very odd event even after becoming very old women, sitting before the fireplace in their rocking chairs.

Now, with the barn continuing to shake itself to pieces with every fresh blow from the creature inside, it was nothing more than an interruption of more pressing business.

Fernie whirled, as if the murky nothingness around them could possibly provide any answers, and grew wild with anger at the sight of Anemone, Caliban, and the three nameless shadows, who had kept their distance all this time and still showed no inclination to come any closer. In fact, no; now that she looked, she could see that the nameless ones were actually striding farther away, shaking their dark heads as if to confirm that they'd watched all they could and had made up their minds that Gustav's cause was not worth joining. In seconds they'd be out of sight and no longer potential allies.

Caliban and Anemone seemed to remain undecided for the moment, but they were still specks in the distance that might as well have been a million miles away for all the hope they offered.

That left Not-Roger and his shadow.

Gustav beat Fernie to the question. "You need to tell us about the gnarfle."

Once again, the crazy tangled forms of Nebuchadnezzar and Cousin Cyrus skipped along the ground in their midst, kicking and gouging and insulting each other as if there were no other concerns worth talking about.

Not-Roger said, "Aren't you more concerned about the fight between your two shadow friends?"

"They're not friends," said Fernie, "and—"

She stopped speaking with the word *and* as another rattling kick or punch or just random assault from the gnarfle left a huge lightning-shaped crack snaking along the entire barn wall.

Gustav continued for her: "You said it's your pet. Can you control it?"

"Gnarfles are not the kind of pets you *control*," Not-Roger's shadow said. "They're the kind of pets you *feed*."

Fernie had one of those, too, the black-and-white house cat Harrington, but she feared that his independent ways weren't exactly the kind of uncontrollable qualities Not-Roger's shadow meant.

Another earsplitting bellow from inside the barn led to another smash and another piece of the wall flying off. The barn looked like it now had only minutes of life remaining to it.

Pearlie wondered out loud, "Will it hold him?"

Not-Roger provided a sad shake of his head. "No enclosure in or out of the Dark Country can possibly contain a gnarfle once it wants to get out. They're the most dangerous predators there are, to creatures of both light and dark."

After only a few weeks of adventures with

Gustav Gloom, Fernie had already grown weary of being told that every new monster they faced was worse than all the ones before it. "We've already defeated something that ate shadows once."

"Not quite," said Gustav, who could sometimes get picky over details at the most inconvenient times. "I mean, it was called a shadow eater, because that's what it filled its belly with, but not because it wanted to eat them. It didn't, really. It just imprisoned them and put them to use for its own purposes. I—"

Another bang rattled the barn wall, and the lightning-shaped crack spawned a number of smaller but somehow even more worrisome cracks, rippling from ground to roof like open wounds. The barn no longer looked like it had five minutes of life left to it. It would be lucky to last two.

Not-Roger's shadow spoke quickly to cut Gustav off before he went further into his explanation about the creature he and Fernie had already disposed of. "Gnarfles don't eat shadows, either. They wouldn't want to, anyway. They don't have throats or stomachs. But they do have flat blunt *teeth* that they like to chew things with. A hungry gnarfle can catch a slow-moving shadow, or one who's been fed to him as punishment, and *chew* him for a long time . . . like what the people in the world of light would call weeks or months or years."

Pearlie's eyes widened. "Like gum."

"Well, yes. I'm told it's highly unpleasant."

The gray blur composed of Nebuchadnezzar and Cousin Cyrus bounced by again, this time in the opposite direction. Cousin Cyrus had his hands on Nebuchadnezzar's eyeballs, which he'd stretched out of their sockets like rubber bands. Nebuchadnezzar had turned his hands into scissors and was cutting at Cousin Cyrus's body, making holes that filled in almost as soon as they were made. All of this was visible in a glimpse before the blur rocketed into the air high above and became a roaring storm cloud, made up of two figures that couldn't stop calling each other names.

Gustav glanced away from that battle, which he couldn't do anything about right now, and returned to the problem of the gnarfle. "What about flesh-and-blood people? Do gnarfles chew them, too?"

Not-Roger brightened, as if happy for the

chance to relay an interesting fact. "Oh sure. A gnarfle will chew anything. But a person wouldn't live through the experience for years, the way a shadow would. A person would be pretty much goo after the first couple of gnashes."

Pearlie said, "I'm beginning to think this is a very stupid place to have this conversation."

Clawed fingers emerged from one of the bigger cracks in the wall and started ripping at the wood to enlarge the hole. The hand itself must have been the size of the barn door. Each of its twelve fingers would have been frightening enough just because of their size, even without the glowing red eyes blinking in the same spots where human beings have fingertips.

All in all, it was the kind of sight that made it easy to understand why this creature was called a gnarfle. Some names just fit, and the possessor of that hand couldn't have been called anything else.

Fernie took a single step back, knowing that it was silly because she could have broken into a run and still not gotten a safe distance away before whatever was left of the barn collapsed into wreckage. "I don't want to be chewed," she said. "There's got to be something we can do.

How did you even catch this one in the first place?"

"Not by being brave," said Not-Roger, whose sun-deprived complexion had gone even paler at the sight of those red-eyed fingers. "I'm afraid that the only way to catch a gnarfle is to find one that's just fallen asleep and build a barn around it while its eyes are still closed. You do the job right and it'll feel so cozy in there that it'll sleep for centuries, as long as nobody makes enough noise to disturb it. The Dark Country's dotted with barns where people keep their sleeping gnarfles. It's just the way things are done here."

Fernie's preference for things that made sense might have suffered mightily during her strange friendship with Gustav Gloom, but was still very much alive. "Okay, so once you have it locked in a barn, just how lonely do you have to be to then *consider it a pet* and go on *living next to it*?"

Not-Roger looked hurt as he spread his massive hands in apology. "The Dark Country can be a lonely place. And as dangerous as they are, they look really, really cute when they're sleeping."

Fernie was still digesting that and trying to determine the best possible way to express just how appalling she found it when Gustav, inexorably moving on to the next mystery, asked, "Is that why it's so important that nobody ring the—"

That's when the roof of the barn blew off.

The entire curved roof, loosened by the gnarfle's restless thrashing, flew off the four walls that supported it and fell to fragments in the air. Planks rained down like spears, one embedding itself in the earth not six inches from Fernie's toes. She dove for safety and came within an even narrower margin of being struck by another. Smaller splinters the size of toothpicks rained down on her back, stinging her through her shirt like darts.

She knew more were coming and would have buried her head in the dirt to avoid the rest as best she could, but there were walls being ripped down behind her. So she scrambled to her knees and then to her feet and *almost* took the first step in the latest in a series of runs for her life.

It was only *almost* because Gustav yelled, "Fernie! Stop!"

Only for Gustav—and, okay, her father and mother and sister—would Fernie have paid attention and *not* run when an insatiable monster and an exploding house were involved.

It was a good thing she did, too, because the next thing to embed itself in her path was the bell.

It didn't look like any bell Fernie had ever seen. For one thing, it wasn't cracked like the Liberty Bell in Philadelphia. For another, it wasn't cast of metal or shaped all that much like a bell at all. It resembled a skull with empty eye sockets and grinning teeth, and it smoldered like something that was trying to decide whether to burst into flames or not. She wouldn't have recognized it as a bell at all if it hadn't tolled the instant it struck the earth, with a thick reverberating clang that knocked Fernie off her feet and left her gasping amid a shower of splinters.

Not-Roger emitted the kind of howl that a man can only make when he's seen all hope destroyed before his eyes. "You rang it! Oh no, you rang it! We might have been okay if it was only the gnarfle we had to deal with! But now we're in so much trouble that being chewed could only be an improvement! We're doomed!"

Fernie was just about to ask what could possibly be more troublesome than being

chewed—being blown into bubbles, maybe?—
when the last remains of the barn fell to pieces.

A shape rose from the wreckage.

Up until now Fernie had thought she'd
encountered the most frightening shadow
monster ever in the form of the People Taker's
pet, the Beast.

But the Beast had been far too vague a thing
to focus on or to see as real.

The gnarfle, by comparison, was a very
specific thing. It was almost all head, and its
head was almost all mouth. The mouth was
too cavernous a space to allow any room for a
stomach or intestines farther in, making it easier
to believe that it was a creature that couldn't eat
but could instead only chew. There were too
many square teeth for the space, piled up in
all directions as randomly as a deck of dropped
playing cards.

Instead of the eyes that one would expect
to find farther up on its head, there were two
smaller mouths that snapped open and shut
and open and shut with a hungry scraping click
each time. They didn't look any more capable of
digesting what they chewed than the big mouth
did, but Fernie knew at once that it would be

just as unpleasant to find herself bitten by them.

Where a normal head would have had ears, the gnarfle's head instead possessed two stubby arms that each ended in giant twelve-fingered hands that also opened and shut and opened and shut as if they couldn't bear the prospect of a moment spent not grabbing and mangling something.

Fernie had already noted the glowing red eyes the gnarfle had on the tips of its fingers, but discovered now that they were even more horrible when they all rolled in one direction and that direction happened to face her.

She shrieked the only thing that came to mind. *"Gustav! The Dark Country is really, really stupid!"*

She was given a moment's reprieve as the entwined forms of Nebuchadnezzar and Cousin Cyrus slammed into the ground between her and the monster, then saw where they were and split apart to run in opposite directions.

The gnarfle blinked its many eyes, as if it found this interesting.

Then it advanced. Despite legs that were as short as its arms, it cleared the wreckage of the barn wall with no difficulty at all, scrambling up the small mound of debris and descending the other side without losing so much as a single step.

Gustav and Pearlie and Not-Roger and Not-Roger's shadow and (much farther away) Anemone all screamed for her to run, but Fernie knew as surely as she'd ever known anything that if she wasted time standing up and choosing a direction and even starting to run away that she would immediately be grabbed by those giant hands and find out what it was like to be *chewed*.

So she did the only thing she could.

She groped blindly for something to throw and by sheer luck came up with a long jagged splinter of wood about the size and shape of the stakes the heroine of her all-time favorite television show had used to carry into battle.

It would have been nice to believe that this piece of wood would prove as effective against gnarfles as her heroine's stake was against vampires, but Fernie could feel that it was already ragged and splintery and would almost certainly break in half if she tried to stab the monster with it. It was a pathetic weapon. Really, it was almost a useless one.

The gnarfle stopped before her, the eyes on the tips of its great twelve-fingered hands

peering at her with the same kind of interest
Fernie would have given a nice slice of pizza . . .
the kind, she supposed, with the extra-chewy
crust.

Then those hands swung toward each other
and Fernie in a blur, intent on trapping her
between them before popping her into that
giant mouth.

Fernie did the last thing any daughter of
a world-renowned safety expert would ever
normally be expected to do.

Instead of running away from the danger,
she ran toward it.

The giant hands clapped shut behind her,
missing her but also cutting off all escape as
she dove screaming at the gnarfle, aiming her
pathetic useless stick at its face.

CHAPTER TWELVE
A MOUTH OVER SHADOW'S INN

Nothing had ever given Fernie any reason to doubt that her sister loved her, or for that matter that Gustav Gloom treasured her as well. But had she harbored any doubts at all, they would have been put to rest forever by the shared sound of their cries during the fraction of a second when it must have looked like the gnarfle would be able to grab her.

The cries stopped as she reappeared, unchewed and no longer carrying her pointy stick, running across the top of the gnarfle's clasped hands.

The gnarfle bellowed and spun, jabbing its massive fingers at its teeth in the manner of any crazed beast objecting to recent developments. The pointy stick protruded from between two of its teeth, stuck there like a flagpole planted in soil.

As Fernie landed back on her feet on ground still strewn with debris from the barn's shattered wall, she saw that things had changed a little in the second or two she'd been busy. Gustav had turned a shade that was pale even for him. Pearlie had clasped both hands to her mouth in fear. Not-Roger had fallen to his knees in shock. His shadow had retreated a short distance and was only now turning around to see what Fernie had done.

The shadow companions Anemone and Caliban were now in their midst, having finally made up their minds to come over and take part in the chaos. There was no sign of the three nameless ones. While it was impossible to tell what Caliban was thinking, Anemone's delicate features had contorted into a mask of fear.

Fate also provided an update on the last two members of the party not accounted for, in the form of a furious gray streak skipping along the ground. Cousin Cyrus and Nebuchadnezzar were once again tangled in mortal combat, still punching and kicking and biting and scratching with a fury only possible for creatures who couldn't really do each other any permanent damage. In a second or two they had again faded into the distance, but Fernie had no doubt they'd be back.

Anemone, who seemed on the verge of tears, cried, "Fernie! *What did you do to the gnarfle?*"

"Gave it something to chew on!" Fernie yelled as she put some more precious distance between herself and the thrashing gnarfle. "It won't last long! We have to run, or hide, or *something*!"

Not-Roger didn't get off his knees. He just shook his head and cried, "That won't do any good! The gnarfle's not your worst problem right now. You rang the bell!"

"I didn't ring the bell! I was on the ground and the bell almost landed on me!"

"It doesn't matter *who* rang the bell! It only matters that the bell was rung!"

Behind her, the gnarfle emitted a furious roar and advanced again. Fernie only knew it had resumed the chase because with each step it crunched broken wood beneath its feet, but the sound was enough to remind her that arguments of any kind were best pursued outside the reach of unstoppable monsters who wanted to chew her. She yelled, "Come on!" and started to run, trusting in her friends and the suddenly oddly concerned Anemone to follow her.

She didn't run away from the inn, as no other direction offered any hiding places. She just ran back toward the front door. The inn wouldn't be able to keep out the gnarfle, but it could provide a few precious seconds of concealment while they huddled together and figured out what to do.

As she reached the open door, she looked over her shoulder to make sure Gustav and Pearlie were following her, and saw to her horror that they weren't. Only the shadows Anemone and Caliban had followed her. Gustav and Pearlie and Not-Roger's shadow were still back at the wreckage of the barn. Each had grabbed hold of one of the kneeling Not-Roger's arms and together were struggling to pull the great bear-size man to his feet.

The gnarfle, still poking at its mouth with its horrid twelve-fingered hands, didn't seem in any immediate hurry to grab any of them, but was thrashing about violently enough to grind any wreckage in its path to powder. The extra fanged mouths it had instead of eyes on its head continued to snap open and shut hungrily.

Anemone grabbed Fernie by the wrist. Her touch was like cold silk, so soft and insubstantial that it was barely a touch at all. "Fernie, dear! They'll either come or they won't! You have to save yourself, at least, or your father's lost!"

Fernie yanked her hand out of Anemone's grip, which was not horribly difficult given that Anemone was a shadow and Fernie's hand was able to pass right through her. Freed, she was ready to run back to her friends and certain death, but then she saw that she no longer had to. Their tugs and pleas had succeeded in coaxing Not-Roger to his feet and getting him to lumber along beside them as they raced for the same open doorway where Fernie stood.

"Inside!" Not-Roger cried. "Inside!"

Nobody needed any additional persuading. They all fled inside, slammed the door shut behind them, and made their way back to the same shabby living room where Not-Roger and his shadow had told the tragic story of Hans Gloom and Howard Philip October to Fernie and Pearlie. Anemone, Caliban, and Not-Roger's shadow didn't need to breathe, of course, but Gustav, Fernie, Pearlie, and especially Not-Roger were all gasping, their eyes haunted at the thought of how close they'd all come to being chewed.

Not-Roger and his shadow sank onto the stools they'd used before, while Fernie and Pearlie took the two others meant for people. Gustav remained standing for the moment, though he didn't look like he very much wanted to. Anemone and Caliban hovered.

Not-Roger spoke first. "You don't need to worry about the poor dear coming after us right away. Gnarfles are all appallingly stupid. He's probably already forgotten that he just saw us run inside. We won't be safe from him forever, though. It won't be long before it occurs to him to start gnawing on the house."

"That's no consolation for Cousin Cyrus," Fernie said. "I may not like him much, but he's proven himself one of us . . . and he's still out there, fighting Nebuchadnezzar. Either one of them could be snatched by the gnarfle at any time."

"True," Not-Roger's shadow admitted. "But there's nothing any of us can do for him right now. When two shadows get into a fight that vicious, it's almost impossible to separate them until one wins or loses."

"Sort of like cats," Pearlie said.

"Or human beings," Gustav said, a dark look

in his eyes. He was probably remembering the story of his father and Howard Philip October.

Anemone did everybody the tremendous favor of breaking the silence that followed. "Fernie, dear? I've never seen anybody, human or shadow, get away from a gnarfle when it was that close. I didn't think it could be done. I know you couldn't have done it serious damage with that little piece of wood. What did you do, exactly, dear?"

It was exceedingly odd for the uncommitted Anemone to call Fernie "dear," but Fernie skipped asking her why and offered an answer instead. "The only thing that stops me from eating when I'm too hungry to stop is getting something stuck between my teeth. It's one of the most annoying sensations I know. When something gets stuck, I suck on it and probe it with the tip of my tongue, and if it's really hard to get at I use a toothpick or my fingernail on it, and I don't start eating again until I get it out. I hoped a gnarfle would act the same way."

Anemone gave Fernie the same kind of look Fernie would have given a dandelion that started singing "Happy Birthday." "So your big plan was to leap at a gnarfle's mouth, hoping to embed a sharp stick in between two of his teeth?"

Fernie shrugged. "I didn't have any better ideas."

"It's not something I would have thought of," Gustav said with admiration. "I don't have all that much experience with food."

Not-Roger's stool creaked under his bulk as if he somehow weighed more than he had the last time he used it. "It was a brave and clever thing, miss. If we had a future, I'd look forward to telling your story to all my future guests. But we don't. *The bell rang.*"

Gustav said, "I think it's about time somebody explains why that's so important."

Not-Roger sighed. "Well, you've got to understand, in the old days anybody who built a barn around a gnarfle always installed a bell tower above it as well. It would never ring a note unless the gnarfle broke out, and when that happened the toll could be heard for miles and miles around, alerting all shadows in range that they should run for the hills in order to avoid being *chewed*."

This was the first element of the Dark Country's odd arrangement involving barns and gnarfles that had succeeded in making even a lick of sense to Fernie so far. "So?"

"So there aren't nearly as many gnarfles as there used to be in this region due to the great gnarfle plague a few centuries ago . . . but bells don't die of plague, so there are just as many of those lying around hither and yon. Lord Obsidian put out the order that they can also be rung to alert his forces of runaway slaves, either human or shadow. Our problem is that, while the Rarely might not be visited very often and my little inn's always been considered beneath his notice before, it's still technically within the territory he's managed to conquer. Considering how fast shadows move in general and the even faster vehicles Lord Obsidian has invented for them, I can't imagine it would take one of his patrols more than a few minutes to answer the call. They'll drag us all off to his vile mines."

Fernie suddenly had absolutely no trouble understanding why Nebuchadnezzar had tried to get at the bell. He might have been chased off for a while back at the Gloom house, but after all this time he was still pursuing his old mission for the People Taker: capturing the What family for Lord Obsidian.

Gustav said, "It might not be so bad. If they arrive and see the gnarfle running around, they'll figure it was what set off the bell and probably want to leave in a hurry. They might miss us entirely."

"Like the bunch that got Dad missed me," Pearlie said.

Not-Roger's shadow replied, "That they might, miss. But they might also check the house just to be sure, and would it really be all that tremendous an improvement for us if they got sloppy, overlooked us, and left us here with the gnarfle?"

Gustav considered that. "No, it wouldn't. But you said they'd probably be here in minutes?"

"Yes."

"By ground or sky?"

"Probably sky," said Not-Roger.

"Good," said Gustav.

Fernie had heard that tone of voice from him a couple times before, most notably on a long and danger-filled night some time ago when he'd explained the difference between coming up with an *idea* and coming up with a *plan*. An *idea*, he'd explained then, comes first, and is what you have when you've first thought of something that might work. A *plan*, he said, always comes later, and is how you're going to make it happen.

From the purposeful way he ran from the room and down a narrow hallway leading toward the part of the house Cousin Cyrus and Nebuchadnezzar had wrecked during their battle, Fernie could tell the *idea* had already occurred to him. Maybe he had a *plan*, too.

Not-Roger's shadow broke the silence that followed Gustav's departure. "It would have been nice if your friend first took a second to tell the rest of us what he was up to before he leaped into action like that."

"I'm used to it," Fernie said, immediately realizing that she actually was. "Come on!"

She pursued Gustav down the corridor, catching a glimpse of him as he turned right at the next corner and left at the corner after that. By the time he had made three course changes, Fernie heard other footsteps behind her and knew that, as expected, Pearlie and Not-Roger had followed as well. She was in too much of a hurry to look back to see if Anemone and Caliban and Not-Roger's shadow were still with them, but didn't see how that mattered, even if Anemone had fallen into the odd habit of calling her "dear."

The inn seemed to have more space on the

inside than its outside would suggest, but not in the manner of Gustav's home, where that actually happened to be true, but rather in the way that certain old rambling houses have. The areas Gustav ran into were even dustier, emptier, and more poorly built than the living room had been, looking like they'd never been used at all and therefore raising the question of why they'd ever been built in the first place; probably because Not-Roger had had nothing but time on his hands and so many years to fill that he had to keep building to avoid going mad.

Gustav headed up a wildly askew flight of stairs, all cracked and broken and tilting to the right in a manner that suggested it had either been built to look like that or been knocked out of alignment by the fight between Nebuchadnezzar and Cousin Cyrus. He seemed to want the location where the two battling shadows had broken through the wall, and as he burst into a room littered with wreckage from the shattered walls and marked with an especially big crater leading out into open air, he stopped, peering upward.

As the others all bunched up behind him, he pointed upward. "There they are."

Fernie saw nothing special: just the dark gray, ominous cloud cover that the Dark Country had for sky.

Then she noticed a small spot, no bigger to her eye than a single speck of dust, growing larger as it approached.

In less than a second, it looked the size of the sun at noon in the sky over Sunnyside Terrace. Then the size of an apple held at arm's length. Then the size of a Frisbee.

By then, she could discern its form. It wasn't round, but rather cylindrical. For some reason that must have made sense to its designer, Lord Obsidian, it curved downward on both ends, like a frowning mouth. Maybe he was so determined to wipe out all joy in the Dark Country and on Earth that even the vehicles used by his servants had to look unhappy. Maybe it was just the shape that worked best. But either way, it was up there, and it seemed to sneer down at the people and shadows hiding inside the inn as if it deeply disapproved of their existence.

Gustav turned to Not-Roger and asked, "Is that the vehicle you were talking about?"

Not-Roger had gone back to sounding like all the hope had gone out of his world. "Yes.

That's one of Obsidian's slave ships, all right. It's a zippalin: like a blimp from the world of light, only designed to move as fast as a jet plane."

Gustav nodded. "Thanks for confirming it. Meanwhile, have the rest of you noticed that it's approaching us from *that* direction," he pointed toward the zippalin, "and we last saw the gnarfle outside the inn in *this* direction?" He pointed back downstairs. "They might not even be able to *see* it from where they are."

Before anybody could absorb this, he stepped up to the great big hole in the wall and started waving and yelling.

"HEY! YOU BIG FAT STUPID MINIONS! WE'RE DOWN HERE!"

CHAPTER THIRTEEN
THE HOLE IN THE WALL GANG

What followed this bizarre behavior on Gustav's part was a fine demonstration of just how much faith the What girls had in him.

It was especially impressive in the case of Pearlie What, whose capture by Nebuchadnezzar and current ordeal in the Dark Country had both occurred after Gustav made one of his all-time biggest mistakes by promising her father that a short visit to his house would be safe.

The girls would only do what they did now, instead of asking Gustav just what was wrong with him, if they still trusted him.

But they did, and so they jumped up and down and hurled abuse at the approaching zippalin.

Fernie yelled, "YOU STUPID MINIONS! YOU ONLY WORK FOR LORD OBSIDIAN BECAUSE YOU'RE TOO UGLY TO GET A BETTER JOB!"

Pearlie, remembering a line from a funny movie she'd been so determined to permanently commit to her memory that she'd once watched it five times in one day, hollered, "YOUR FATHER WAS A HAMSTER AND YOUR MOTHER SMELT OF ELDERBERRIES!"

"What a distinctly odd thing to say," murmured Not-Roger's shadow. "Is smelling of elderberries even a bad thing?"

Up in the sky, the zippalin pivoted like a turning face and appeared to consider the noisy and quite possibly mad denizens of the inn.

Vertical lines dropped from its belly, not making any sense to Fernie until she realized that they were climbing ropes spun from shadow-stuff, stored aboard as coils and released by the crew whenever they wanted to descend and attack something. Two dozen shadowy forms began to descend those lines, moving with the speed of creatures who had no bones to break and therefore didn't have to worry about getting hurt if they lost their grip and fell.

"COME ON!" Gustav hollered. "WHY ARE YOU ALL MOVING SO SLOWLY? ARE YOU SCARED WE'LL BE TOO MUCH FOR YOU?"

One of the minions had already descended far enough for his voice to be audible. "Oi! Just 'oo do you think you're talking to, you little meat bag?"

The minion released his line and tumbled toward the wreckage of the barn, landing there in a puff of dust before standing again to face the inn with a triumphant and evil grin. He was a particularly misshapen shadow, with tiny legs, a massive chest, and a head that would have gotten any art student working with modeling clay thrown out of class for not having the slightest idea what a head was supposed to look like. "Oi'm gonna enjoy seein' this one in the mines. Silly mugger don't know well enough to keep his mouf shut!"

More of his fellow minions also released their lines and sank gently to the ground. One landed right next to the first and beamed with the shadow equivalent of big, greasy, food-encrusted teeth. "We'll teach him that, Scrawbers, we will, we will! He'll learn to bend the knee!"

A dozen shadow minions now stood inside the wreckage of the barn, looking eager for the brutality to come.

As they left the field of debris and began to approach the inn's only door, Gustav murmured, "Here, gnarfle, gnarfle, gnarfle . . . !"

The gnarfle seemed to hear him, because that's when it came lumbering around the corner of the inn and met the nice collection of chewable items who had just dropped from the sky in its vicinity.

A couple of the minions still descending from lines screamed like the littlest of little girls and began scrambling back up. Those on the ground were taken by surprise and were frozen with fear for the heartbeat or two it took for the monster to scoop two of them into its cavernous mouth.

The openmouthed way it chewed reminded Fernie of a boy named Lester Funmuntz, who had sat in the desk next to hers at the last school she'd attended. Lester had chewed gum nonstop, and any moment where his mouth happened to be shut and his wad of gum not visible to everybody in his vicinity could not be described as anything but a fleeting accident. Otherwise his jaw continued to flap and gnash as wide as the hinges of his skull allowed. The only real difference between the gnarfle and

Lester Funmuntz was that chewing gum never actually objected to being chewed, and the two shadow minions in the gnarfle's mouth did little else. They howled and screamed and yelled "Ow! Ow! Ow! Ow!" and scrambled to escape and begged their friends for rescue and generally, in all possible ways, raised the biggest fuss possible.

"I almost feel sorry for them," Fernie said.

"They're minions of Lord Obsidian," Gustav replied. "How sorry for them are you willing to be?"

One of the other minions on the ground, evidently a loyal sort, made a halfhearted attempt to grab the outstretched arm his friend had managed to extend outside the reach of the gnarfle's teeth for a moment in order to pull him free. Instead, he was shoveled in himself. The chorus of anguished shadow minions being mangled between the gnarfle's teeth increased by one. "Ow! Ow! Ow! Ow! Ow!"

Anemone shook her head. "This, dears, is why I said it was particularly dangerous for beings of my kind to go anywhere near that barn. The presence of too many shadows can drive gnarfles into a kind of frenzy."

Fernie was about to snap that the immediate

neighborhood didn't seem any safer for human beings, either. But then two more minions descending from the zippalin swung through the gaping hole in the wall and into the room, rendering that the kind of argument that didn't have to be made.

The one with the beak nose and the tiny pinprick eyes waved his scimitar and cried, "By all the soup of the abyss, this looks like it will be a mighty haul! Meat and traitor shadows both!"

The other was a pig-faced shadow whose jowls and fat lips shook like jelly beneath eyes like bottomless pits. "And not just that, Scabby-Tongue! Don't you see the treasure we've found here? That's a little boy in a black suit! *That's Gustav Gloom!*"

The pig-faced jowly one lunged for Gustav, who as always managed to be just out of reach when someone with evil intent grabbed for him. He snarled and reached for Gustav again, only to find himself wrestled aside by the hooded Caliban, who seemed to have made up his mind that he was actively involved in this fight whether he wanted to be or not.

The two shadows struggled. Caliban and the jowly pirate teetered at the edge of the hole in the inn wall and might have fallen either way depending on how their battle went, but then two giant twelve-fingered hands reached up from below and plucked the pirate from the air. In an instant, the jowly shadow had joined the writhing mass of unwilling shadows being chewed in the monster's mouth.

It was harder to see what had happened to Caliban, as he'd fallen from sight, and in the instant his fate became unclear, Anemone cried out, *"No!"* Her features seemed to shift, the fresh face of the young woman whose shadow she seemed to be giving way, her cheeks becoming puffier and wider. It was only a second before she became herself again, but the slip had been enough to establish what Fernie had begun to suspect: that, like Olaf, she was not the person she'd been pretending to be.

Scabby-Tongue cried out in anger at the chewing of his friend. "You meat bags! I don't care what Lord Obsidian's offering for you! He can have you after you've been chewed awhile!"

He lunged for the nearest human being, Pearlie What.

Pearlie threw a punch that landed squarely on his nose. This staggered him a little, even though her fist passed through his nose without making any measurable impact.

Scabby-Tongue drew back his shadow scimitar and slashed it across Pearlie's midsection. It was such a mighty swing that, had his sword been a solid object instead of a shadow, Pearlie might have been cut in half. This would have been a somewhat more serious prospect for a human girl than it had been for Cousin Cyrus. But she only looked confused for a moment. Then she grinned with the realization that she hadn't been hurt and punched the beak-nosed minion in the face again. "We can't hurt each other! He's *nothing*! I could do this all day!"

Fernie would have liked that to be true, but she remembered her encounters with other shadows and knew that they could be as solid as they wanted to be at any time. "Don't be overconfident! They—"

She was too late. Scabby-Tongue had solidified enough to seize Pearlie by the neck and lift her struggling form off the floor.

He might have gone through with his threat and tossed her out the hole in the wall for the gnarfle to chew, but Gustav took advantage of his temporary solidity and kicked him in the behind. Scabby-Tongue hopped up in the air a little, dropped Pearlie to the floor, and whirled on Gustav, who simply kicked him again, this time in a place where nobody likes to be kicked. Fernie finished the job with a powerful shove, which propelled Scabby-Tongue out the hole in the wall.

Like a character from an old-fashioned cartoon, Scabby-Tongue seemed to hang there for a moment, surprised that two children had succeeded in landing such effective hits.

Then Caliban's hand rose up and grabbed him by the ankle to yank him over the edge.

The gnarfle leaped to pluck him out of the air, and Scabby-Tongue found himself part of the increasingly unhappy mob being chewed in the monster's mouth.

"Ow!" the writhing shadows in the gnarfle's mouth cried. "Ow! Ow! Ow! Ow! Ow!"

Caliban pulled himself back through the hole in the wall to rejoin his allies in the shattered room. "Glad to be back," he said, more cheerfully than anything he'd said for as long as they'd known him. "I'm so glad that I didn't end this day being chewed."

For the first time, Fernie got the impression

that he wasn't exactly who he'd been pretending to be, either.

Pearlie rose to her feet, rubbing her bruised neck. "I hate to say it, but this isn't going all that badly, considering. How many shadows can that thing chew at once without having to spit any out?"

"Gnarfles don't spit *anything* out," Not-Roger's shadow said. "I've heard of single gnarfles catching and chewing the population of an entire shadow city, all at the same time. It's not like there wouldn't be enough room in his mouth. It's a big mouth, and shadows can be crunched down pretty flat, once they're chewed enough."

"What happens to them, if they can't ever die? Can they escape?"

"You're a kid," Not-Roger said, pointing out what Fernie would have considered obvious. "Have you ever gotten so excited running around and doing kid things that the gum in your mouth falls out by accident? Now imagine all your gum kicking and screaming and trying to get out. Imagine a couple of dozen separate pieces of gum in your mouth at the same time, all fighting to get out while you're so busy trying to catch more gum that you can't pay proper attention to your chewing. It might take hundreds or even thousands of years, but they'll all find their way out, even if they then have to take time to smooth out all the bite marks."

"The Dark Country isn't just stupid," Fernie announced. "It's gross."

"That it is," said Caliban. "Given a choice, I much prefer the world of people."

Unfortunately, the break in the fighting was now over. A dozen more shadow minions, including four indistinct ones with no human features and a bunch of others who must have spent their time on Earth being the shadows of phenomenally ugly people, swung into the room waving shadow swords. More shadow minions bunched up behind them, until they all blended together into a thick gray fog. There seemed to be almost twenty of them now, all flashing cruel grins, all eager to add the humans and shadows before them to their haul.

The gnarfle leaped again and seized two entire handfuls, but there were more descending minions than even he could catch or chew before the crowd at the hole in the wall became an actual threat.

As they advanced away from the edge and out of the gnarfle's immediate reach, Gustav cried, "Everybody retreat!"

The What girls didn't need any further coaxing. Fernie and Pearlie barreled out the door of the room behind Gustav and Anemone and Caliban. Not-Roger followed them only as far as the doorway, which he filled, swinging his massive arms at the dark shapes that threatened to bury him. Because they wanted to be solid enough to seize him, he actually succeeded in knocking a few down with a swing and even tossing a few the length of the room and out the hole in the wall for the gnarfle to seize and chew. With his shadow fighting at his side, Not-Roger bellowed, "This is my inn! These are my guests! You . . . are . . . *not* . . . welcome . . . here!"

Farther down the hallway, Fernie peered over her shoulder to see if there was anything she could do to help them. But no, even during the one glimpse she could steal, they were buried beneath a mass of writhing gray bodies. One of the black lines from the zippalin entered the room, moving of its own accord like a snake, and wrapped around Not-Roger's midsection, pulling his screaming and cursing form from sight. Not-Roger's shadow went down under a pile of other shadow minions. Then the hallway behind Fernie was so clogged with advancing black shapes that she could see no more.

Anemone shouted, "Fernie, dear! Come on!"

"Your name's not Anemone!" Fernie retorted. "You're Great-Aunt Melli—"

Another black line whipped around Anemone's belly and pulled her up short. Her face shifted again, and this time confirmed what Fernie had figured out: that Anemone was Great-Aunt Mellifluous, the shadow who had become the closest thing Gustav had to a mother after the disappearance of Penny's shadow when he was five.

There was no time to ask her why she had hidden her identity or pretended that she had not yet decided to help Gustav and the girls on their quest. For that matter, there was no time to ask the next logical question: who Caliban was if he, like her, was shrouded in disguise. By then he had gone to help Anemone and was busily trying to free her from the black line when another one whipped around him and imprisoned him as well. He only managed to fight the black line long enough to cry, "Don't give up! You're not alone!" Then the lines yanked both Anemone and Caliban back and they disappeared into the advancing mob.

Fernie cried, "There are too many of them!"

"I'm aware of that," Gustav said, as always a million miles away from panic. "I expected a manageable group, not the small army we got."

Now at the bottom of the stairs, Fernie slammed a door shut behind her, knowing that it would not keep their pursuers at bay for long. "So what are we going to do?"

"Get captured, I expect."

Fernie and Pearlie both started yelling at once. *"But Gustaaaav—"*

"But then," he said, keeping up his explanation even as they barreled down the long twisty hallways back to the room where Not-Roger did all his entertaining, "I knew that much before we even started. Think about it. We *need* to get captured."

Pearlie started screaming at him. "What do you *mean* we need to get captured?"

That wasn't all she yelled. She yelled some things that were horrible and others that would have been unforgivable in any other circumstance. She yelled with a level of anger that was only reasonable, considering that it came from a girl who had successfully escaped the Dark Country once and had returned with him out of faith that he knew what he was doing and would make sure that everything turned out all right. Now she was even worse off than she was before and about to be captured by Lord Obsidian's minions, only to hear Gustav announce that it was all part of his plan.

This is exactly the kind of thing that makes people who'd already been through a rough time carry grudges.

Fernie, on the other hand, froze, focusing on the other thing he'd said.

Think about it.

She thought about it and realized to her dismay that Gustav was right. He was more right than anybody she'd ever known, even if what he was right about happened to be too terrible.

They *had* to be captured.

The Dark Country was just too vast a distance to cross otherwise.

Being captured was the only way for Gustav and Fernie and Pearlie and the shadows traveling with them to get where they wanted to be, past all the land's monsters and death traps and hidden dangers, without either getting themselves killed or giving up their whole lives to the task of passing its perils alive.

Fernie had no way of knowing whether Gustav had a *plan* for what to do when they got dragged before Lord Obsidian or just an *idea*, or if all the plans and ideas were over with. She had no way of telling whether all that awaited them was the same lifetime of slavery they would have suffered if they'd just tried a little bit harder and gotten themselves captured later on. But she felt a terrible calm descend upon her, like a warm quilt on a cold night.

Gustav was right. This was the only way.

She thought all of this in a second and came to her decision as they burst into Not-Roger's living room, the horde of shadows just a couple of steps behind them. Pearlie was still yelling at Gustav for not having any plan other than just letting themselves get captured. Fernie silenced her sister by placing a cold hand on her wrist.

Pearlie skidded to a stop, shut her mouth, gave Fernie a wild-eyed stare, and then, meeting her eyes, horribly, *got it*. "Oh no. Really?"

Fernie said, "Really. For Dad."

Pearlie gulped, shook her head as if wishing something could possibly make what was about to happen go away, then turned the head shake into a despairing and angry nod. "Okay." She glanced at Gustav. "For your dad, too. And this better work. If we don't eventually get a happy ending out of this, I'll never talk to you again."

Gustav was unruffled. "Don't worry. I like you too much to let that happen."

"Okay," said Pearlie.

The swarm of shadow minions burst into the room. There were hundreds of them, too many to fight. The ones with faces looked cruel and calculating, and the ones without faces looked like something out of the nightmares Fernie hadn't had since she was six. Just looking at them, she felt a lot smaller, and a lot more helpless, than she'd ever felt when she was six.

"Let's at least make it look good," said Gustav.

"Let's not," said Fernie. "Let's make it look great."

Clutching hands, screaming at the top of their lungs just to give themselves courage, Gustav, Fernie, and Pearlie ran together out the front door of Shadow's Inn.

CHAPTER FOURTEEN
A GNARFLE WAY TO END THE DAY

Heroic gestures are a fine thing in theory.

But as soon as Gustav and the What girls were out the door, it occurred to Fernie that as long as they had been resigned to being captured anyway, they might have been better off just waiting around and letting it happen inside Shadow's Inn.

This would have been easier, for one thing, and it wouldn't have required them to get back outside, where they'd last seen Cousin Cyrus and Nebuchadnezzar and where the gnarfle was still running around, grabbing up handful after handful of shadow minions and popping them into a mouth that was already as crowded as a train station at rush hour.

"Ow!" the shadow minions in its mouth cried. "Ow! Ow! Ow! Ow! Ow!"

The landscape in front of Shadow's Inn

teemed with shadow minions, waving shadow scimitars and shadow axes and rushing about in panic as the gnarfle ambled about among them, like a restaurant patron taking an all-you-can-eat buffet too seriously. Its mouth was now gummy with mangled, barely recognizable shadow forms, all bearing highly visible tooth marks and most distorted into curlicue knots from the ordeal of being chewed. Shadow arms and shadow legs dangled from what would have been its lips, had it possessed any lips.

"Ow! Ow! Ow! Ow! Ow! Ow!"

Pearlie What was the first of the three friends to be captured. A long black line from the zippalin snaked down from the sky, seized her by the ankles, and yanked her off her feet. She was not pulled into the air right away for some reason, and instead was swung along the length of what remained of Shadow's Inn just a few feet off the ground.

Fernie ducked under a minion's shadowy sword thrust and ran after Pearlie, intent on rescue. Another minion tried to tackle her by the legs, and she simply leaped over him, rolled, and went on, her fingers inches from Pearlie's outstretched hands. She didn't focus on those hands, but instead on her sister, with her wide eyes and shiny forehead and gaping mouth. Then she put on a burst of speed, seized Pearlie's hand with her own, and ran behind her for a while, unable to do anything but keep up.

Then the black line yanked Pearlie skyward. Fernie felt her own feet yanked off the ground as she held on to Pearlie with all her might, and for a fraction of a second thought that it might be okay to just hold on, stay with her sister, and let herself be dragged all the way to the zippalin with her.

But Pearlie was not about to risk Fernie's life by attempting to hold on to her younger sister at a great height. She dug her fingernails into Fernie's palm, forcing her to let go.

Fernie tumbled to the ground, scraping her knees and elbows upon landing. She could only look up helplessly as Pearlie screamed down at her, "It's okay! Keep running!"

Pearlie receded into the sky, becoming first a smaller version of herself, and then a dot, before she was gone.

Counting two occasions back at Gustav's house, this was the third time Fernie had seen her sister taken away from her. It was not an experience she'd enjoyed all that much the first two times, and it did not much improve with repetition.

She whirled around, searching for Gustav. She spotted him an amazingly far distance from the house, staying ahead of a small mob of shadows who didn't seem to be able to surround and catch him no matter what they did. It must have been a terrible novelty for these minions to find themselves pitted against a halfsie boy who was as hard to catch as the most slippery shadows were.

But Fernie had proven herself hard to catch more than once, and she wasn't about to be captured any more easily than he was. So when dark forms gathered around her, she darted through the one hole in their ranks and ran in the one direction none of them would have guessed that she was willing to run.

She ran screaming toward the gnarfle, which was just stomping through all the chaos, scooping up one shadow minion after another and shoving them into its toothy and already overpopulated maw.

The screams of the shadows already being gnashed and chewed between those teeth were about as terrible as anything Fernie had ever heard.

They were upset and put-upon and frightened. Quite a few of the shadow minions cried out for their mothers, which would have been an interesting development at any other time, as Fernie had never once in her life suspected that shadows *had* mothers. She supposed, distantly, that this only made sense, as she'd already met one who identified herself as a great-aunt.

But she didn't have any more time to think about it, because there it was, just up ahead, its twelve-fingered hands flexing and grasping and reaching out to her.

She threw herself to the ground.

Just above her head, the shadows who'd been chasing her screamed as they overshot her and found themselves within the gnarfle's grasp. It stepped over her to get at them, seizing them out of the air and ramming them into its mouth in writhing bunches.

It *chewed*. It chewed *noisily*. It chewed *wetly*. The only reason Fernie couldn't accuse it of bad table manners was that there was no table in sight.

It also hummed while it chewed. It was a happy gnarfle.

The wadded-up shadows in its mouth yelled, "Ow! Ow! Ow! Ow! Ow!"

Another black line came rolling down from the sky, intent on grabbing her the way another had grabbed Pearlie. Fernie was tempted to just save herself some time and trouble and let herself be taken, but she wasn't ready to let that happen yet, not when she'd just spotted something that interested her very much only a short distance away.

She would never be able to say how she managed to spot this one thing out of everything else she had to occupy her attention, but she did spot it, and the sight was enough to make her curl her hands into fists as she rose to confront what she saw.

A very long time ago, Fernie's mother had shown her a funny old movie about a bunch of silly people racing around the world. At one point, they stopped in a distant country where a bunch of even sillier people found themselves having a violent disagreement in a bakery. Everybody started throwing pies at everybody else's faces. It was very funny to watch what felt like thousands of custard pies flying back and forth and for both good guys and bad guys to get splattered with cream. But the most important part of the scene was the way the hero of the movie walked through the door and for a while quietly walked through the center of the madness without being hit by a single pie.

Fernie knew what it must have been like for the hero of that movie. She was in the center of even greater madness, in a battle populated by what felt like hundreds of shadows flying back and forth to catch her while also trying to avoid being caught by the gnarfle. There was also Gustav Gloom, who had retrieved one of the rapiers and was currently doing a fine job keeping at least six of the minions at bay in a heroic duel she honestly would have liked to see more of if she hadn't had something more important to do.

But none of this touched her. None of it even came close to mattering as she walked through it all toward the spot where, alone and almost as untouched by the battle as herself, Nebuchadnezzar knelt.

The shape-changing shadow, responsible for kidnapping her father and sister in the first place and for bringing all this current trouble on by disguising himself as a friend, already looked like he'd been through a war. He had transformed back into his favorite disguise, the helpless little pigtailed girl, but seemed to be having trouble maintaining it. There were holes in him, holes that went all the way through him and would have allowed daylight to pass through him had there been any daylight nearby that wanted to do such a thing. The little girl's face was mashed all to one side.

Cousin Cyrus looked almost as messed up as Nebuchadnezzar. He lay on the ground at the shape-changer's side, keeping a tight grip on his enemy's wrist while continuing to throw his weak punches.

"Let go," Nebuchadnezzar complained as his face crumpled again from yet another punch from the not-quite-defeated Cousin Cyrus. "There's no point in fighting me anymore, you stupid old coot. You've lost. Lord Obsidian's minions have come and the foolish children are doomed."

"Not . . . as long as I . . . still owe . . . debts . . ."

Not far away, a tiny shape flew into the sky, dragged upward by another of the zippalin's black lines. It was Gustav, who had either figured that it was time to be captured or had been captured against his will before he was entirely ready to go. He didn't cry out, so Fernie took what satisfaction she could in pretending to herself that he'd given up deliberately.

She wasn't worried, because she had every intention of seeing him again very soon.

His capture just meant that she had only a couple of heartbeats before the remaining shadow minions took stock of what still needed to be done and all came for her, gnarfle or no gnarfle.

The dust the fight had stirred up seemed to be shielding Nebuchadnezzar, Cousin Cyrus, and Fernie from the minions for now, but to her it didn't seem to be the main reason why none of them were coming after her right now. No, she was being left alone, seemingly invisible to everybody right now, even unseen by Nebuchadnezzar though she was only a few feet away from him.

Sometimes, she thought, things happen in a certain way only because they have to.

"Cousin Cyrus," she whispered.

Nebuchadnezzar whirled. He hadn't heard Fernie approach at all.

Cousin Cyrus scowled up at her. "What . . . do you want . . . from me now, girl? Haven't

I . . . already done . . . enough for you brats?"

"Yes," she said. Time seemed to have slowed down, and all doubt in her appeared to have fled. "You've done everything you had to. I can't release you from any debts you owe to anybody else, but speaking as Pearlie's sister, I release you from the debt you owed her. You don't have to punish Nebuchadnezzar anymore. You can let go of him. And I thank you."

"It's about bloody time," Cousin Cyrus muttered, releasing Nebuchadnezzar so he could flit off into the distance and smooth out his own dents in peace.

Nebuchadnezzar's little-girl eyes widened in astonishment as he rose from the dirt to face down the angrier and somehow far more fearsome little girl before him. "What on earth would you do that for, you foolish little—?"

Fernie punched him in the face.

It was an ineffective blow, in that she was a very solid girl and he was at the moment about as easy to strike as a rain cloud. Her fist passed through him harmlessly. But he had been through a lot already in the last few minutes, and instead of doing the smart thing and simply flitting away leaving only scornful laughter behind him, he made a terrible mistake and did what Fernie had somehow known he was just angry enough to do. He snarled and turned solid enough to punch her back.

The blow landed on Fernie's shoulder instead of her face. It knocked her half a step back, but that was okay. She'd been willing to take the punch and any pain that came with it in order to have something solid to grab. This she did, seizing Nebuchadnezzar by the wrist and pulling him with her as she spun around and started running, with him held before her at arm's length.

Nebuchadnezzar still had enough time to slip from her grip, turn into anything he wanted to be, and fly away triumphant. But he did none of these things. He was too paralyzed by the look in her eyes, and possibly by the same sense Fernie had, that this was exactly how the history between them had to end. "No! No!" he cried. "You can't! It's too cruel! I don't want to be *chewed*!"

The gnarfle was now just a few feet away, its giant mouth chomping up and down as its terrible hands spread wide apart to grab its next treat.

Fernie had just enough time to say, "Then you should have left my family alone!"

Then she threw Nebuchadnezzar at the gnarfle's hands.

He changed shape at least four times before the gnarfle's massive hands slammed shut, catching him. He became the little girl from the Hall of Shadow Criminals who had so sweetly promised to be Fernie's friend. He became the version of Gustav Gloom he had once pretended to be, the one who was mean and cruel and who Fernie had not liked at all. He became the friendly shadow of an ancient knight called Olaf, who according to legends had defeated entire armies with his terrible stench. And then, just before the gnarfle captured him, he became the shape that was probably closest to his true nature: a thin, hollow-eyed nothing of a man who did evil things because he wasn't special enough to do anything better with his life.

It was in this last shape that he entered the gnarfle's mouth screaming.

Then the big flat teeth came down and rose back up and came back down again, turning Nebuchadnezzar into something that reminded Fernie of what she saw whenever her sister tried to disgust her by opening her mouth to display a pile of thoroughly chewed French fries.

The only difference, of course, was that the French fries wouldn't have been yelling at the top of their lungs and begging for mercy.

"No! No! Save me! Please! Ow! I promise I'll be good! I'll be your friend! Ow!"

This was the cruelest thing she had ever done to anybody, and it didn't feel bad at all.

In fact, it felt pretty good.

Then one of the black lines from the zippalin came down, whipped around her waist, and yanked her into the sky.

She may have been the only human being ever captured by them who went smiling.

EPILOGUE
LAST STOP BEFORE THE REAL MONSTERS

The word *meanwhile* doesn't make a lot of sense in this situation, because the Dark Country and Sunnyside Terrace are two different worlds entirely, and time doesn't exactly work the same way in both places. These things can be hard to measure.

To people living on Sunnyside Terrace, the hours had passed at about the same rate they always passed. The sun had set and the first stars had started to shine in the deep indigo sky. Most people had started settling in with their televisions, a much smaller number with their books, and a smaller number still with other diversions.

The door of the Fluorescent Salmon home opened, and Nora What stepped out. She was still dressed in the same safari jacket, jodhpurs, and pith helmet she'd been wearing when the cab dropped her off at home earlier that day, the same clothes she'd worn when she'd read the strange letter from the younger of her two daughters and when her own shadow had spoken to her and driven her into a very undignified faint. She looked a little pale for a woman so tanned by the sun, but her eyes were set and focused, and her brows were knit together in a single furious line. She was gone from home a lot because of her job, but nobody who knew her had ever said that she wasn't a mother.

As she crossed the street and headed toward the Gloom house, she passed under the streetlights, revealing that there was only one shadow with her: her own. There was no visible sign of Fernie's shadow, or Mr. Notes's shadow, or Hives. But the backpack she had donned bulged in odd ways, and anybody standing close to her would have discerned impatient shushing noises coming from within.

None of her neighbors were around to see this. This was not entirely a good thing for her, since if she'd had the chance to meet or speak to any of her neighbors, they might have told her what she'd missed while lying unconscious after her faint: that this had been a very odd day at the Gloom house. Strange lights had flickered in the usually dark windows, the walls had rumbled from noises that sounded like every item of furniture in the house shattering all at once, and a number of shadows had simply fled out the front door and drifted down the street, anxious to be anywhere but there. It all added up to an odd and disturbing afternoon around a house that was sufficiently odd and disturbing already.

Unfortunately, the only neighbor talkative enough to insist on telling her all this, one Mrs. Adele Everwiner, was currently in her car and breaking all the speed limits fleeing to her sister's home in another state. So nobody told her. The information wouldn't have stopped Mrs. Nora What even if somebody had told her, but it would have been nice to be warned that things at the Gloom house had changed for the worse.

She entered the property through the open gate and made her way across the foggy front lawn to the pair of giant front doors. She took a deep breath, gathered her courage, and knocked.

A distant voice inside cried, "Hold on! I'm coming!"

She waited. Then she waited some more. Then she waited longer still.

A man opened the door. His eyes and his smile

were far too big for his face, and he was so pale that he probably should have spent some more time in the sun, but other than that he looked friendly enough. He wore a green button-down shirt decorated with a pattern of bananas, red parrots, and big tall drinks with little umbrellas in them. He said, "Sorry it took so long! I was in the game room, way on the other side of the house. How are you today?"

Mrs. What suddenly felt very silly. "Hello. I'm—"

"No," the man said, "let me guess. I think I know who you are. I've seen your TV specials. You're Nora What, right? Fernie's mom! It's such a pleasure to meet you! I'm your new neighbor, Brad Gloom!"

"Thank you," Mrs. What said automatically, because it was what she always said whenever anybody told her they knew her TV specials. Then she said, "I've just come back from Africa."

"Have you?" Brad Gloom exclaimed. "How charming!"

"Very," Mrs. What said, cutting off the inevitable questions about where she'd gone and what she'd done. Then she said, "I'm looking for my family?" phrasing it as a question.

Brad Gloom was, of course, not named Brad Gloom at all. There was no Brad Gloom. The man standing before Nora What was better known by now, to the other members of the What family and to the shadows of the Gloom house, by his title, the People Taker. He happened to be a very dangerous person, more monster than man. But as far as appearances were concerned, he was Brad Gloom, who looked faintly ridiculous and, more importantly, completely harmless in his banana-and-parrot-and-umbrella-drink shirt.

Brad Gloom said, "Oh right. I'm sorry, they're inside. We've been having so much fun in the game room that we must have lost all track of time. Today was the day they were supposed to go to the airport to pick you up, right?"

"Right," said Mrs. What.

"I bet they'll be perfectly horrified when they find out. Come on in. I'll take you to them."

Mrs. What hesitated, perhaps in response to the rustling noises coming from her backpack, some of which came very close to sounding like whispers. After a moment, her eyes turned awfully cold for such a nice woman being offered help by someone she was supposed to consider a friendly neighbor. "Thank you."

Less than five seconds later, the doors closed behind her, and night on Sunnyside Terrace returned to silence.

The slave hold of the zippalin was a place of oppressive gray fog, half-insane muttering from huddled figures behind iron grates, captive shadows swirling in cages of pure light, and the cruel laughter of minions taking joy in the misery of the tears of those they'd captured.

"Don't worry," said the massive round-shouldered minion using the tip of a shadow spear to prod Fernie What along a creaking walkway to cells in the darkest depths of the ship. "It may not be the luxury your lot is used to up there in the world of light, but ye won't be in your cage for long. We've got special orders for your little band and will be delivering you directly to the castle of our master before you know it."

"That's a relief," said Fernie. "I was afraid I'd have to wait a long time. I didn't bring anything to read."

"Ye'll wish ye'd been given the option to wait, my pretty. Being a slave in his mines is like a nightmare that never ends, but being delivered to Obsidian personally is a frightful thing that happens only to the unlucky few. I hear tell he has enemies who have fed themselves to gnarfles rather than get within a hundred leagues of him. If I were you, I'd save meself some time and start howling for mercy now." He cackled. "It won't help, of course, but there's no sense putting such things off to the last minute. You—"

"I wish you'd just shut up and put me in my cage already. You're boring."

This seemed to hurt the fat minion's feelings a little, probably because it was the one big speech he ever got to say and he'd put so much work into honing it for the greatest possible fearsomeness that the worst possible thing any prisoner could do was shut him up in the middle of it. He grumbled to himself, no doubt finishing up all the really ominous bits under his breath, then directed Fernie to a set of ugly steel boxes with mesh windows and padlocked doors. Another cackling minion who crouched atop those boxes, playing idly with a spear, undid the lock so the fat one whose feelings Fernie had hurt could toss her in.

She landed on a floor covered with something she supposed to be the Dark Country's equivalent of straw, even if it didn't feel much like straw and didn't smell much like straw and was the very last thing she'd want to dangle out of her mouth when she was wearing a farmer hat on a warm summer day. It was not a big cage. She'd hoped for a reunion with Pearlie here, but it looked like this cage was meant for her and her alone. Just in case, she called out, "Pearlie?"

"Over here," said Pearlie through a slot in the wall separating Fernie's cage from the one on her immediate right. Any tears she'd shed since leaving Shadow's Inn could no longer be heard in her voice, and she seemed to be taking the same attitude Fernie had taken: sheer impatience for the next bit. She asked, "What took you so long?"

"I was busy feeding Nebuchadnezzar to the gnarfle."

Pearlie was silent for a moment. "You know, I am so deeply sorry I missed that."

"I'm sorry you missed it, too. It was everything I hoped for. Where's Gustav?"

"I'm over here," said Gustav Gloom from the cell on the other side.

A more distant voice, coming from a cage a

farther distance away, complained, "I'm here. Thanks for asking." This was Not-Roger, who was understandably in a bad mood after having his barn torn down, his pet gnarfle set free, his inn destroyed, and his freedom taken away from him.

"I'm here, too," said Caliban, and now his voice sounded nothing at all like the cold, empty thing it had been when first they'd met him.

"Me, too," said Not-Roger's shadow.

"And me," came Anemone's voice from somewhere else nearby. After a pause, she added a careful, "Dear." Fernie couldn't help noticing what she was meant to notice, that this last word was not delivered in the vibrant tone the shadow had used as Anemone, but the rather richer and sweeter notes she had used as an older woman named Great-Aunt Mellifluous. It was a subtle difference, and only when the two voices were used one right after the other was it impossible to avoid noticing how alike they were, and how clearly they were now revealed as the voice of the same person at different ages.

Fernie wished she understood everything that was happening, but for now she shuffled over to the thin slit in the wall that separated her cage from Gustav's and asked him, "What about you? Are you okay?"

"F-fine."

Nothing that had happened in the last couple of hours worried Fernie more than the tremble in Gustav's voice. If Gustav Gloom broke down, that meant Gustav Gloom could stand no more . . . and if Gustav Gloom could stand no more, then the faith in him that kept her own courage up now dangled by a very thin thread.

Suddenly afraid, she tilted her head to peer at him through the slit and saw him sitting quietly in a dark corner of his cage, his pale face as hard to see as a thin cirrus cloud drifting across the sky on a cold moonless night. Something on his cheeks glistened.

"Gustav!" she cried. "Are you all right?"

"What?" To her surprise, Gustav was genuinely puzzled by the question. "Why wouldn't I be all right? I thought I told you, we needed to get captured. We wouldn't have ever gotten anywhere if we weren't captured. This"—he waved to indicate the cage and gave a little extra wobble of his fingers to include the zippalin and all the vile enemies who surrounded them—"all of this, is okay. I've been in worse places."

Fernie wondered if he was just pretending to be braver than he was in order to make her feel better. "You're not worried?"

"Of course I am. We have so much left to do. But I don't think it's anything we can't handle. We'll be okay."

She decided he wasn't trying to fool her. He might have been wrong about their ability to survive it, because he'd been in danger so many times in his short life that it was almost impossible for him to accept that any dangers could possibly be too much for him. But at least he was not faking his confidence. That he felt, and because he felt it, Fernie could feel it with him.

Still, there was that one nagging question. "Why are you crying, then?"

He tilted his head, then raised a finger to his cheek and brushed at the glistening wetness there. "Oh this." He didn't speak again for several seconds, and when he did, his voice was unusually soft and quivery. "It's nothing. It's just that . . . since being caught, I've had time to think about where we're going and what we're going to find there, and . . . well, it's not a bad thing, really, but I've been sitting here, and . . .

you know, it feels real to me for the very first time."

"What?"

He moved closer so she could see him. His eyes were red and his cheeks moist, but for the very first time since she'd met him he wore a smile that had nothing to do with defeating an enemy or tasting a chocolate chip cookie.

She realized what he was about to say just before he said it, and understood that the tears welling in his eyes had nothing to do with fear or grief.

He said, "I think I'm going to get to meet my father today."

Fernie understood now, but understanding made her have similar thoughts about her own father, and how good a man he was, and how great it would be to see him again, even in a place as robbed of hope as the Dark Country. She wiped her tears with the back of one hand and slipped the other as far as it would go through the wall slot until Gustav found her fingertips with his own.

Together, in silence, they waited to find their fathers.

ACKNOWLEDGMENTS

You would not now be seeing this book without the persistence of agents extraordinaire Joshua Bilmes and Eddie Schneider of the Jabberwocky Literary Agency. You would not now be enjoying the same experience free of verbal land mines and other clutter without the ace red pens of copy editor Kate Hurley and editor Jordan Hamessley. You would not now be oohing and aahing over the illustrations without the genius of artist Kristen Margiotta. You would not now be holding the divine artifact in your hands without designer Christina Quintero. You might have no idea the book exists without the fine work of publicist Tara Shanahan. You would not now be seeing any books from me at all without the patience, love, and constant encouragement of my beautiful wife, Judi B. Castro. You would not now be seeing a human being with my name and my face were it not for my parents, Saby and Joy Castro.

I must give an extra shout-out to a man who died long before I was born, who for various reasons I probably wouldn't have liked very much: Howard Philips Lovecraft, the extraordinarily influential writer who is the distant inspiration for the villainous Howard Philip October, and whose Cthulhu Mythos stories left a large footprint that can be felt various places in the lands that Gustav and Fernie visit.

ADAM-TROY CASTRO has said in interviews that he likes to jump genres and styles and has therefore refused to ever stay in place long enough to permit the unwanted existence of a creature that could be called a "typical" Adam-Troy Castro story. As a result, his short works range from the wild farce of his Vossoff and Nimmitz tales to the grim Nebula nominee "Of a Sweet Slow Dance in the Wake of Temporary Dogs." His twenty prior books include a nonfiction analysis of the Harry Potter phenomenon, four Spider-Man adventures, and three novels about his interstellar murder investigator, Andrea Cort (including a winner of the Philip K. Dick Award, *Emissaries from the Dead*). Adam's other award nominations include eight Nebulas, two Hugos, and three Stokers. Adam lives in Miami with his wife, Judi, and three insane cats named Uma Furman, Meow Farrow, and Harley Quinn.

KRISTEN MARGIOTTA has been creating spooky, creepy images since her early childhood. Now as an adult, she explores similar themes with more depth and further enjoyment. Since her graduation from the University of Delaware in 2005, she has been working as an artist, illustrator, and art instructor within the Delaware art community. Kristen finds that her different roles as a visual artist and instructor influence and strengthen each other, and she enjoys the challenges and rewards that come from these endeavors. Kristen is the illustrator of the picture book *Better Haunted Homes and Gardens*, and her work can be found in the homes of collectors throughout the country. She has exhibited her paintings and merchandise regionally and in the Southwest through galleries, museums, and local events. Learn more at www.kristenmargiotta.com.